James Grant

The Girl He Married

A Novel. Vol. I

James Grant

The Girl He Married
A Novel. Vol. I

ISBN/EAN: 9783337027117

Printed in Europe, USA, Canada, Australia, Japan

Cover: Foto ©Andreas Hilbeck / pixelio.de

More available books at **www.hansebooks.com**

THE GIRL HE MARRIED.

A Novel.

BY

JAMES GRANT,

AUTHOR OF "THE ROMANCE OF WAR," ETC.

"O! good, your worship, tell it of all things; for I mightily delight in
hearing love stories."
SANCHO PANZA.

IN THREE VOLUMES.

VOL. I.

LONDON:

TINSLEY BROTHERS, 18, CATHERINE ST., STRAND.

1869.

CONTENTS.

CHAPTER VII.

CHAPTER VIII.

CHAPTER IX.

CHAPTER X.

CHAPTER XI.

CHAPTER XII.

CHAPTER XIII.

CHAPTER XIV.

CHAPTER XV.

CHAPTER XVI.

CHAPTER XVII.

CHAPTER XVIII.

CHAPTER XIX.

CHAPTER XX.

CHAPTER XXI.

CHAPTER XXII.

CHAPTER XXIII.

THE GIRL HE MARRIED.

CHAPTER I.

BY THE NIGHT EXPRESS.

THUS ran the brief but startling telegram which was delivered late in the evening :—

" Dr. Feverley, Blairavon, to Lennard Blair,
Liverpool.

" Come home by the first train. A crisis is at hand. Your father cannot survive much longer.

From Liverpool to Blairavon, in Scotland, is more than one hundred and sixty miles by rail, the only mode of conveyance now, and poor Lennard Blair thought nervously of his chances of being at home in time to see—before the fatal moment—that parent to whom he was so tenderly attached ; and in a rapid and bewildered manner, acting as one might do in a dream, he thrust a few necessary articles into a carpet bag, preparatory to starting by the night express train for Carlisle and the North.

I.   B

He glanced at his watch; he had already lost two
hours, during which the telegram had been waiting
for him, while he had kept several business engage-
ments between the counting-house and the Hus-
kisson Dock.   In those two hours what might he
not have lost! and from amid the bustle of Liverpool, and the roar of its busy streets, his memory
flashed home to his father's secluded mansion in
Lothian.

To Mr. Abel Envoyse, the managing clerk or
cashier of Messrs. Vere, Cheatwood, & Co.—a meek-
looking little gentleman with a bald head, who had
been in the house for years upon years, who had
never set up for himself, and never hoped to do so,
whose ambition was probably satisfied by the salary
now given him, and who thought Vere & Cheatwood
the greatest firm in the world, even as Liverpool
was the centre of the universe—to Mr. Envoyse, we
say, Lennard Blair intimated the pressing nature of
the telegram he had received, and that he must start
at once for Scotland.

Though a clerk in the establishment, and one who
had to work hard at his desk, Blair had a few
thousands invested with the firm, and ranked as
a junior-partner therein, but his name did not
appear as such, so Mr. Envoyse felt himself compelled to consent, in absence of Mr. Vere, for
Cheatwood and the Co. had long been myths.

"You will complete those bills of lading for
Leonardo & Co., of Vera Cruz," said Blair, with
nervous haste, "and I shall see Mr. Vere about
other matters, when I reach Scotland; he is there

before me. Meantime, I require, please, a hundred pounds in gold."

" Gold ?" echoed Envoyse, rubbing his bald head.

" Of course; English notes are useless in Scotland."

"Past bank hours. Do you want the money now?"

" This instant."

The sum was large for one in Blair's position.

" We never keep much in the house when Mr. Vere is away," said the old cashier, reluctantly unlocking one of Milner's great patent safes; " but here you are, Mr. Blair."

" Thanks," and even in his haste, so strong was the force of business habit, Lennard counted over the money, and gave a receipt, while muttering in a broken voice, " I am telegraphed for, because my poor father is—is dying."

" Good bye, Blair," said some of the clerks, with all of whom he was an especial favourite.

" Wish I was going with you," added one, who was an idler, and usually wished himself anywhere but at his desk.

" But not on such an errand, surely," said Blair, as he thrust several dockets of papers into his drawer, and locked it.

" Oh, no, my dear fellow, I didn't mean that," replied the young man, colouring, as he bent over his ledger, on which the gas-jet cast a glare from under its conical green shade.

The counting-house of Vere, Cheatwood, & Co., was then in an alley off Canning Place, and in the immediate vicinity of the Revenue Buildings, the Custom House, and Post Office, admirably situated for business, and in the most bustling part of the quays.

Lennard Blair sprang into a passing cab, and "tipped" the driver.

"To where, sir?" asked the man.

"Terminus—Great Howard Street—go like lightning, my good fellow!" and the short distance between Canning Place and the station of the Lancashire line was soon traversed, yet scarcely quick enough for the impatience of Lennard Blair.

The first bell had already been rung; the carriage-doors were being slammed to; the last of the luggage was being tossed into the guard's van, or hoisted on the roofs, and pointsmen and porters were running hither and thither, as Lennard hurried along the crowded platform, looking for a seat.

He had not been without hope of getting a carriage, or rather a compartment thereof to himself, that he might indulge in his own melancholy reflections, undisturbed by the presence of strangers, the thoughtless, perhaps, and the noisy; but the first glance he gave along the train dissipated the expectation; the carriages seemed crowded—every seat apparently was engaged.

Though far from being a sordid character, Lennard Blair had been more used latterly to travel by second, and even third class, than first; and now, when paying for the latter, he had certainly no desire to endure the useless discomforts of either of the former. The guard saw that he was carrying his own bag, and so left him to shift for himself.

In the centre compartment of a first-class carriage sat a young man, with long, fair moustaches. He was alone, and dressed in a fashionable travelling suit, with an eye-glass screwed into the rim of his white half-bullet hat, and through this optical medium he was leisurely surveying the bustle on the platform, and about the departing train.

Thrice had Lennard attempted to open the door, but found it locked, for the person in possession of the entire compartment had doubtless a private key.

"Engaged here," said he briefly, yet Lennard saw that he was alone, the five other seats being vacant.

"Are you sure, sir?" asked Lennard anxiously.

"Quite—all engaged here."

"Awkward, excessively. I have looked everywhere else for a seat."

"Ah! then you may do yourself the pleasure of looking again; there is just time," was the chaffing response, as the other drew up the window-glass to cut the matter short. He then unfolded *Punch* and the *Times*—placed his hat-box on one cushion, his carpet-bag on another, some rugs on a third, his umbrella on a fourth, his feet on a fifth, and himself personally on a sixth, proceeding thus, like a free-born Briton, to occupy as much of the premises as he could, to the exclusion of others.

Not a vacancy was to be seen elsewhere. The up-train from the north was panting and puffing outside, its red lights glaring in crimson along the line; the guard was swinging his lantern, and shouting "Tickets! have your tickets ready," near the last carriages of the train.

"Guard," said Lennard, slipping a couple of florins deftly into that official's back-turned hand; "get me a seat, please, anywhere!"

"Which class, sir?"

"First."

"Plenty of room, sir, in the centre compartment of the third carriage; five seats unoccupied; look alive, sir, please."

He of the eyeglass and long moustaches, who had been watching Lennard's anxiety with some amusement to himself, had again lowered the window, as the gas-lighted station was close and dense in atmosphere, and the night—one of the last in April —being warm and without a breath of wind. Moreover, the supervisor of the tickets had thrown open the door now.

"Sir," said Lennard, emphatically, when he saw that in addition to other lumber, books and papers now strewed all the cushions, "are those seats really engaged?"

"Don't you see that they are?" drawled the other.

"Now, this one, for instance?" urged Blair.

"By whom?" added the guard.

"Can't tell—by *Punch*, and my hat-box, I suppose."

Lennard seized the articles indicated, and tossing them far out on the platform took possession of the seat, and throwing some of the rugs, &c., from the opposite one underfoot, proceeded to make himself at home.

With an angry oath, he of the eyeglass, who little anticipated so summary a proceeding, sprung out to recover his property, and had barely regained his seat, being roughly shoved in by the guard, when the bell rang, the shrill whistle cleft the air under the lofty iron roof of the station, out of which the train glided away between Great Howard Street and the Leeds Canal, while Lennard Blair and his fellow traveller, by the light of the carriage-lamp, eyed each other with glances the reverse of friendly.

" If we are to travel together, considering your insolent disposition, you will be none the worse for being snubbed, my fine fellow," thought Lennard.

" Curse him; some post quill-driver, or bumptious snob, out on the loose, I suppose," muttered the other, almost audibly, while stroking his moustaches with an angry and supercilious air.

" Did you think, sir, to occupy the whole carriage ? " asked Lennard, whose cheek glowed with an emotion of indignation, which certainly served to repress his sorrow and anxiety.

" The whole carriage—well, perhaps so ! "

" And may I ask why ? "

" Because in this world every man has a right to get as much as he can for his money, and I always take deuced good care to look after Number One,' he replied, coolly.

He then began to whistle a low but popular street

melody, while Blair busied himself with his "Brad-shaw," that volume obscure apparently as the shastres of Brahma, inextricable as the hiero-glyphics of Memphis; and through all the mazes of Parliamentary and express trains, of first, second, and third classes, the charges for cattle and luggage, &c., he sought to reckon over the anxious hours that must inevitably intervene before he reached Blair-avon in Western Lothian.

This young man in his four and twentieth year, wearing the grey Tweed suit and smart wide-awake hat, pray observe him well, friend reader, for he is the hero of our story.

His hair is a rich curly brown; his eyes are neither brown nor grey, yet there are times and lights in which they seem both; with clean-cut features, he is closely shaven, all save a thick moustache; he has a straight nose and handsome mouth. His figure is strong and lithe, every muscle being developed, as with bat and oar and rifle he has kept his place among the best in England, and is moreover the champion shot of the Liverpool Volunteers.

Blair's voice is very pleasant, and musical too; there is a singular chord in it, that wins every ear, and seems to speak of a gentle and tender nature, though there are times when he can be bold and stern, but always a manly young man.

Swiftly sped the night express train.

Liverpool, with its mighty world of wealth and work, its wilderness of docks and forests of masts, the broad waters of the Mersey, on whose bosom uncounted lights were shining from ship and shore, from wharf and sea-wall,—all were left behind. The dark masses of the Industrial School and Kirkdale Jail on one hand, the scattered village of Bootle on the other, were soon glided past; houses became more scarce and far between, and after emerging from the long and rumbling tunnel, the train was careering through the open country under the clear and lovely light of an April moon, while Ormskirk with its market-place and coalpits, Farrington and its moss, soon vanished in the distance.

Once or twice Lennard Blair, who had much to think of and to reflect on, turned his eyes from the swiftly passing scenery without to the face of his fellow-traveller, who evidently was neither inclined to converse or make himself agreeable; for barely had the train emerged from the tunnel beyond Bootle Lane when he produced an embossed silver case of great size, and selecting therefrom a cigar (a rat's-tail with a straw through it), he lit it with a flaming vesta and proceeded to smoke without the ceremony of an apology offered or permission given, and without the usual courtesy of offering one to his companion.

This man's features were striking, but unpleasing; his complexion was fair, almost to unhealthy paleness; he wore that species of beard denominated a goatee, and seemed some ten years or so older than Lennard, to whom his whole bearing was eminently offensive, displaying a cool insolence which, if he dared, might verge on open ruffianism; yet his travelling suit, his Albert chain, rings, scarf, and gloves, &c., were all in the most unexceptionable taste.

It is seldom that people take much interest in their fellow-travellers, even though they are to journey all night with them; but now Lennard Blair felt—how or why he knew it not—an intense and intuitive antipathy for this person. There was a strange expression in his pale green eyes which (rather than their form or colour) made Blair recoil instinctively from him; and they had a stealthy and peculiar mode of looking away when those of another met them; yet Lennard felt certain that whenever he affected to sleep or look from the window the gaze of his companion was fixed keenly upon him.

With this emotion of repulsion there floated through Blair's mind some of the many stories he had heard or read of attacks, outrages, snares laid, and even murders committed in railway carriages; but he almost smiled as he felt his own biceps, for he knew himself equal to tossing the stranger out of the window if the occasion required him to do so.

Little could Lennard Blair foresee how much, in a future time, his fate was to be influenced by this cool and impudent fellow who sat smoking in front of him, and superciliously pulling the windows up or down, as suited his own fancy or convenience. Lennard's intuitive dislike at last became so strong, that while surmising whether this personage was one of the swell-mob, he asked :

" Are you going far this way, sir—along the line
I mean ? "

" Rather too far, perhaps," was the dry response.

" How ? "

" Into Scotland," he replied, with a thick and
unpleasant voice, as if his tongue was too large for
his mouth.

" Too far, you think ? "

" To West Lothian, if you know such a place; I
never heard of it before. But here is Preston
already. By Jove! we have come at a ripping
pace ! " he added, as the train swept with a hollow
roar into that bustling and bewildering station,
where so many lines meet and intersect; and then
ensued the usual banging of doors, the clinking of
the hammers on the wheels to test their soundness,
the shouting of newsboys, the swaying of lanterns,
and hurrying to and fro of porters, platform-officials,
and sharp-eyed pointsmen.

" Do we change here ? " asked Blair anxiously,
snatching up his bag to be ready for the answer.

" Of course we do—change for the Black Sea,
Calcutta, and the Baltic," drawled the other, perpe-
trating an old joke, which was meant as impertinence, while he lay back in his seat and watched
the smoke of his cigar rising in concentric curls up
through the ventilator in the carriage-roof.

" Tickets ! " shouted the guard, while a weather-
beaten and well-whiskered face appeared at the
window, thus arresting a threatening gesture made
by Lennard's hand towards his companion's nose.

The smoker now made studiously a delay, to worry and annoy the official, by slowly searching every pocket in succession, as well as his pocket-book, cigar- and card-cases.

"Smokin' is agin the company's rules—a fineable offence; and you should have your ticket ready, sir," said the official.

"Should I really?" drawled the other; "do you want it?"

"No."

"Then why do you bother about it?"

"Because it must be shown and checked," replied the guard, becoming furious, but restraining his passion, as he flashed his bull's-eye full into the traveller's face. "Look sharp, please, or——"

"Or what?"

"I shall call a policeman."

"Don't trouble yourself, my dear fellow; if the pasteboard is worth seeing, it is worth waiting for," replied the other, who, after trying the man's patience to its utmost limits, showed his ticket at last, expressing a hope that the sight thereof "would calm his ruffled feelings and soothe his troubled bosom."

With an imprecation, the official checked the ticket, slammed to the door, and the laugh of the impudent traveller was lost amid the clatter of the train, as it steamed out of the station towards Lancaster.

Full of disgust for such a companion, yet wondering who he might be that was going exactly to the same part of Scotland as himself (T. C. appeared in

large white letters on his portmanteau), Lennard
Blair lay back in a corner of the carriage, and with
half-closed eyes communed with his own heart,
thinking of the sorrows that awaited him, of the
past that had gone for ever, and the anxieties that
might cloud his future.

CHAPTER II.

HOMEWARD ON THE NORTH WESTERN LINE.

ON sped the swift night express by the great
North-Western line, its monotonous hum and
motion being conducive either to drowsiness or
reflection; thus Blair, though he closed his eyes as
if to sleep, permitted his mind to become a prey to
anxious and exciting reverie.

"In the morning of our days," says the eloquent
Burke, "when the senses are unworn and tender,
when the whole man is awake in every part, and the
gloss of novelty fresh upon the objects around us,
how lively at that time are our sensations, yet
how erroneous are the notions which we form of
things!"

Lennard Blair was still in the morning of his
days, yet in some respects he had lived long enough
to see many errors and had won much experience.

He was going back on a sorrowful errand to the
narrow world—the little rural circle from which he
had emerged some five or six years before; and as
the homeward train sped on, faster than the engine,
yea, faster even than the electric telegraph, the posts
of which seemed to be flying past in pursuit of each

other, did his thoughts flash back to earlier years
—the past returned to memory, and the present
fled.

The only surviving son of Richard Blair of Blairavon, he had come into the world with the fairest
prospects of succeeding, if life was spared him, to an
ample, even noble inheritance, which his father contrived, with the utmost assiduity, to squander on the
turf and elsewhere, till the whole of his property,
save the remnant named Oakwoodlee on which he
resided, had, by mortgage, purchase, and otherwise,
passed into the hands of Mr. Vere, the wealthy
Liverpool merchant.

"Home-keeping youths have ever homely wits,"
to quote the "Two Gentlemen of Verona." Lennard
soon learned the truth of this, and resolved to seek
his fortune—or, as his father phrased it, in a moment of bitterness, "to earn his bread"—elsewhere,
having become early aware that nothing was to
be won by a life of dependance on his father's
shrivelled purse; and it was not probable the blind
goddess would seek him out on the pastoral braes of
Blairavon.

He had accepted Mr. Vere's apparently kind offer
of a desk in his counting-house, and invested in the
firm a moderate sum that had accrued to him from
his mother, the heiress of a few hundred acres; and
thus he had gone south to Liverpool, among its busy
thousands, to labour and to learn, to work, to wait,
to make a way in the world, and to regain, if possible, the position and wealth of which his father's
extravagance and imprudence had deprived him;

for Lennard treasured in secret all that pride of name and family which is inherent in the Scottish character, and he shrunk nervously from the conviction that, unless he thus strove, with resolution and thrift, the old Blairs of Blairavon would go down into the common herd (from whence they had sprung centuries ago), and be heard of no more.

Romances which Lennard had read in boyhood, and the prophetic wishes or hopeful prophecies of his old nurse, Elsie Graham, and of his father's attendant, Stephen Hislop, once butler at Blairavon, now valet, groom, and general factotum in the little household at Oakwoodlee, had all conduced to strengthen these honourable fantasies—this earnest, but perhaps desperate ambition, in the young man's heart.

On the Blairavon lands is a grey old Druidical monolith named the Charter Stone. It was a firm belief in the family and county, and had been so for ages, that so long as a Blair retained a right of proprietary in this unsightly block, the race would prosper. Thus a thousand times had the impoverished old gentleman reminded Lennard, with glee, that though "the wealthy *parvenu*, Mr. John Vere," had won the lands of Blairavon "by his sordid and drudging industry," the Charter Stone was on the remnant they still retained near Oakwoodlee.

His father, though he heartily despised all manner of business, and was totally ignorant of it, save in the items that related to bills, kites, and I O U's, had, after gulping down his old family pride, fostered the wish of his son to the utmost. Hence, to buy back the old patrimony, or to create another; to toil, and spin, and work; to emigrate and dig, but only to return and regain the old place that had gone out of the original line, was the object of Lennard Blair, as it has been the Golden Dream, the romantic hope (in *no* instance, perhaps, ever realized), of many a Scottish wanderer in the woods of America, in the Australian bush, the mines of California, and the diggings of Ballarat: but this was the secret impulse which animated Lennard as he drudged at his desk amid the roar of busy Liverpool.

During the first few years he had been in business he had learned much, but had not clambered far up the social ladder. He was literally only a clerk in the great mercantile firm of Vere and Cheatwood, with a small share in the profits derived from the money he had invested in the stock, by the advice of Mr. Vere, whose acquaintance and patronage he had acquired when that gentleman purchased his father's estate.

With all these sanguine hopes and delusive desires, the combined result perhaps of early education and secret vanity, there existed in the mind of Lennard no emotion of upbraiding or reproach against his father. The poor old man was dying now; his weaknesses and his errors were things of the past to be forgotten; his virtues alone were to be remembered; and the last time Lennard had seen his wistful, kind, and saddened face, when he left home to push again on his worldly way, came vividly to memory now.

I.   C

To add to Lennard's troubles, he was in love—in love with Hesbia Vere, his employer's only daughter; a young lady ere long to be introduced to the reader.

As a neighbour when at Oakwoodlee, and as one of the best round dancers and most pleasant friends whom she met at home, Hesbia Vere had always preferred, or seemed to prefer, Lennard Blair to many other young men whose wealth or worldly position were infinitely greater than his. On whose arm could she droop or lean more pleasantly and freely when breathless, flushed, and palpitating after a long waltz or a furious galop; and who so readily found her fan, or bouquet, and so gracefully and deftly cloaked or shawled her for the carriage?

He had brought her beautiful flowers and the rarest exotics; ferns, the most remarkable; a wonderful parrot from a West India ship in the Albert Dock—a parrot that swore most fluently, but luckily in Spanish.

He lost bets of gloves to her so adroitly; selected her books and pointed out passages which, when underlined by pencil, told *so* much more than he would have dared to say; they had exchanged innumerable *cartes-de-visite*, and he had sketched and written in her album more than perhaps Papa Vere would have quite approved; but that was a species of book he never by any chance opened.

They frequently met by the most singular chances in quiet and shady corners of the Botanical Gardens, or when she was riding in the Prince's Park and other promenades. Lennard Blair, in virtue of the sum invested in the funds of Vere and Cheatwood, rather than in consequence of his gentlemanly bearing and good birth, was every way Hesbia's privileged dangler, greatly to the envy of his fellow-clerks, and to the annoyance of several admirers of more pretensions.

He had made love to her in every way that man could do, short of actually declaring it, and in such a way the flirt—for notoriously was Hesbia Vere a flirt—received it.

All this alluring intercourse with the bright and beautiful girl had made more impression on *his* heart than it left on hers; for Hesbia became his sun, his centre, his pole-star; yet he was merely one among many priviliged admirers who hovered about her, especially when he was elsewhere; and it was only a realization of what the old rhyme tells us of the moon that looked on many brooks. So, as Lennard thought of her in his reverie, he whispered to himself,—

"Oh what can ever come of such a passion as mine? In love—in love with one of the greatest flirts in Liverpool? A girl who is vain as she is beautiful, and fickle as she is vain. What folly or magic is it that lures me to become her shadow, when I know that she has jilted and trifled with wealthier, wiser, and better-looking fellows than I? Even her cousin Cheatwood has failed with her, if I have heard aright; and I am to see her again, for she is at Blairavon with her father. She, at Blairavon!"

So pondered Leonard amid his waking dreams

in the night as the train glided on, now through deep cuttings, and then along grassy embankments, where the telegraph wires sung in the wind like Æolian harps; past darkened or half-lighted stations, where the offices were closed, the book-stalls shut, and the platforms deserted; the flaming posters and huge placards on the walls alone remaining to indicate that on the morrow's dawn the stream of life would flow again.

On past red-gleaming furnaces and dark pit-mouths, the clanking engines and whirling wheels, the smoking chimneys and murky atmosphere of the Black Country, where night and day, underground and above it, the brawny gangs of grimy men are for ever, ever toiling; on through the gloom and uncertainties of the scenery, as the moon waned, and white lights and green, or the crimson danger signal, flashed out of the obscurity; past green paddocks, shining pools, and thick hedgerows; past villages buried in sleep; past tall ghostly poplars, and those pollard willows and oaks, the eccentric trimming of which is peculiar to England; past huge manufactories and coal and iron mines, with cones of flame that reddened earth and sky.

And so on flew the train by stately Lancaster, where the stars shone brightly in the depths of the Lune, and on by the picturesque vale of Kendal embosomed among beautiful hills; on by the grassy fells of Westmoreland and the old castle of Penrith, whilom built by Richard of England as a barrier against the Scots—an open and gaping ruin now—and thence onward by Carlisle; and the breaking dawn saw the express train careering through the green and pastoral glens of the Southern Highlands, while the early mists were rising in light grey masses from the grassy summits of the Hartfell, the highest of the Scottish mountains south of Forth and Clyde.

With the aid of his private key Lennard's companion had got out for refreshments—"nips and pick-me-ups," as he styled them—at every station where the train stopped. Blair had no desire to accompany him, but sat wakeful and apparently listless in a corner, full of his own thoughts, which increased in keenness and intensity as he found himself among the mountains and nearing home.

But he deemed it a singular coincidence that, though he changed carriages twice, and twice even to different trains and lines, his unpleasant fellow-traveller was constantly his *vis-à-vis*, and made exactly the same changes at the same times and places.

Influenced probably by the numerous brandies-and-water he had imbibed, this personage now condescended to make some inquiries about the localities they passed through; but as the replies were always followed by sneers, in which he seemed prone to indulge, or by pitiful jests and disparaging reflections on the country, the people and the features, or names of the scenery, Lenuard Blair became irritated by his rudeness, and relapsed into studied silence.

Once he offered the use of his brandy flask to the stranger, by whom it was coldly and curtly declined, and after this he proceeded to use his *own*.

It was now that sweet season, the end of spring, the last few days of April, when the buds have burst in all their freshest greenery in the gardens and woodlands; when the daffodil, the yellow crocus, and the primrose peep up from under the sprouting hedgerow; when the young lambs are basking on the sunniest slopes of the hills, and the swallows are returning from their mysterious flight; when rivulets and cascades are all swollen by the spring showers, and rush down towards the glens with increased force and volume; when "fresh flowers and leaves come to deck the dead season's bier," and a spirit of youth and new life seem in everything.

> "Through wood and stream, hill, field, and ocean,
>   A quickening life from the earth's heart has burst,
>   As it has ever done."

And nowhere is spring more lovely than in our southern Highlands, and on the pastoral braes of Annandale.

Now Lennard Blair was drawing nearer and nearer to his home, especially after he had passed the meadows, the woody haughs, and morasses of Slamanan, an old Celtic name which signifies "The Back of the World."

Last night amid the roar, the lights, the multitudes of Liverpool; this morning in a solitude where the shrill whistle of the curlew, or the lowing of the cattle, as they were startled by the passing train, alone woke the silence!

But this was home, and with eager eyes did Lennard scan the old familiar haunts and features. Every sight and sound woke boyish memories in his saddened heart; the chaunting or whistling of the rustics, as they rode their giant horses afield; the black gleds wheeling in the sunshine from the ruins of Torphichen—that church and fortress where the Lords of St. John of Jerusalem lie cross-legged in their graves, with shield on arm and sword at side; the mountain burn that gurgled under the green whins, bearing last year's withered rushes to the Avon (the dark and winding river), the old church tower in the distance, and all its sheltering groves of beech and chestnut.

In yonder burn-brae had he, aided by old Steenie Hislop, unearthed and killed his first otter; from that pool he had landed his first salmon, and there, amid the black boulders that lay in mid-stream and chafed the waters into white froth, he had filled many a basket with speckled trout in the happy times of boyhood that could return no more.

On yet, and in the distance he could see on the green slope of a hill a great grey monolith upreared in its loneliness amid the pastoral solitude, and then he felt his pulses quicken.

It was the Charter Stone of Blairavon, and it stood, as he knew, but a few furlongs from the house of Oakwoodlee, where his old father lay on his death-bed.

In the middle distance was a stern group of aged Scottish pines—the last remnants of an old forest, coeval with the Torwood, where once had roamed

the snow-white bulls and ferocious bears of Caledonia
—the stems of the gnarled trees standing out redly
from the feathery masses of bright green fern, while
the crags of Dalmahoy and the hill of Logan-house,
the highest of the beautiful Pentland-range, little
less than a mile in height, rose against the clear blue
sky beyond.

The next station was three miles further on than
Oakwoodlee, but the latter was still in sight when
the shrill whistle of the train cleft the morning
welkin. The speed became slower, and tickets
were searched for, and bags, umbrellas, and hat-
boxes were clutched by the passengers in their haste
for release from their temporary imprisonment.

A handsome tilbury, a bang-up affair, with patent
drag, plated axles, and a high-stepping horse, with
splendid harness, was waiting the arrival of Lennard's
companion. The groom was in the Vere livery, and
the Vere crest appeared upon his buttons, the
harness, and ostentatiously on more parts of the
vehicle than one.

With much fuss and obsequiousness, the groom
collected the portmanteaux, rugs, plaids, rods, and
gun-case of the traveller, and had a couple of pointer
"dawgs," as that personage called them, brought
from the guard's van. ·

"How far is it from here to Blairavon?" he
inquired.

"About three miles, sir," replied the servant,
touching his hat; "you'll be there in time for
·breakfast."

"The old boy at Oakwoodlee is awfully cut up, I hear."

" If you mean Mr. Blair of Blairavon—"

" No—you seem jolly verdant for a Scotsman—he that was."

" Oh, sir ! folks say he is dying."

" Poor old fogey; and so his lands have gone to those servants elect of mammon, those worshippers of the golden calf, whom he despised so much."

" They have gone to master, sir," said the puzzled groom, touching his hat again.

" Exactly; jump up, all right," replied the other, assuming the reins and whip, and without a farewell nod or recognition, he drove off, leaving Lennard Blair, who looked somewhat earnestly after him, perplexed and stung by the remarks he had over-heard, to trudge afoot with his bag and rugs, as at that solitary little station there were no vehicles to be had for hire.

CHAPTER III.

OAKWOODLEE.

THE mansion of Oakwoodlee, in which Lennard's father had resided since the loss of Blairavon, had been originally the jointure-house of the entire estate, and was first built for an ancestress, Griselda Blair, of the Tor Hill, whose husband fell at the battle of Dunblane, in 1715, with the white cockade in his bonnet, and a colonel's commission from King James VIII. in his pocket.

It is a plain, small, two storeyed house, with great chimney-stalks, crowstepped gables, and scroll-formed corbels at the corners. The walls are massive: in front are nine windows, set deep into the masonry and whilom grated with iron in former times of trouble. A coat of the Blair arms—the star of eight points, and so forth—is carved above the door, to which a flight of broad stone steps gives access, and which is furnished with a great bell in addition to a ponderous, old fashioned knocker.

In the south-western gable is built an ancient dialstone; the front of the mansion faces the south, on the green slope of a hill surrounded by old copsewood, the shootings of which were always let to add to the shattered income of old Richard Blair.

Before the door is yet standing the identical "loupin-on stane," with its three time-worn steps, by the aid of which Lady Griselda, of Blair-avon, was wont to mount behind her butler on a pillion, when they rode together on one horse weekly to the church of Inchmachan.

At the door he was warmly, even affectionately, received by the two faithful adherents of their fallen fortunes, who had been watching his approach. Old Elsie Graham—once his nurse in youth, and now his father's in old age—a hard-featured, but kindly, old motherly woman, who met him with a scared and anxious face; lips that were white and eyes inflamed by recent tears and long watching.

"Welcome back, laddie! welcome hame! but oh, Mr. Lennard, what a sorrowfu' hamecoming is this for you," she exclaimed, covering her face with her faded black-silk apron. "Oh, sirs! oh, sirs! what is this that has come upon us a' at last!"

"Hush, woman, will you?" said old Steinie Hislop, sharply interrupting her noisy but half-stifled grief; "dinna add to his distresses by your din and non-sense. But I say wi' Elsie, welcome to you, Mr. Lennard, though it be in an evil hour," added the old man as he shook Lennard's hand, and then respectfully hastened to relieve him of his bag, railway rugs, and cane.

"And my father, Steinie," asked Lennard, with a quivering lip, "how is he?"

"More composed now—more resigned to the

great change that is at hand—than when Dr.
Feverly telegraphed for you last night."

Lennard sighed bitterly.

"He is asleep, so dinna disturb him," added
Steinie; "and while you are getting some refresh-
ment, the doctor will join you."

"Then Dr. Feverley is here?"

"Yes, Mr. Lennard; but asleep on the dining-
room sofa. All night was he awake and most
attentive," said Elsie. "But step your way ben to
the breakfast-parlour; fu' well must you ken the
gate, my braw bairn."

"Is it likely I should ever forget it, Nursie?"
asked Lennard, with a kind, sad smile, as he entered
the old familiar room, the windows of which faced
the ancient grove of Scottish pines that cast their
shadows, as they had done for ages, on the charter
stone, while both Elsie and Stephen Hislop hovered
restlessly about him intent on kindness and commiseration; for they had loved the lad from his
infancy, and since their own youth had been in the
service of his family.

Old Stephen, who had latterly been groom of the
venerable Galloway cob (which represented what
was once a noble stud); gardener of the little plot
where a few edibles were grown; valet, butler, and,
as already stated, factotum—still wore a kind of
shabby livery coat, with a striped-blue and yellow
vest, long and flapped, with drab breeches and
gaiters; a kind of hybrid costume between groom
and footman. He was a thin, spare man in his
seventieth year, round-shouldered; with clear, keen,

anxious, grey eyes; thin white hair, and hollow and wrinkled face.

At a glance, Lennard took in the whole details of the room and of its furniture; the full length of his father—a handsome man in hunting costume, with his favourite horse—by Sir J. W. Gordon, was an imposing picture; but the other appurtenances were relics of the "plenishing" procured for his grandmother in the days when George III. was king, and they seemed odd, quaint, and most unmistakably shabby when contrasted with much that he had been accustomed to of late. Yet all were familiar as old friends: the square-elbowed horsehair sofa, with black squabs and pillows; the circular stand for curious old china; the corner cupboard, with its green dram-bottle and worm-stemmed glasses, the teapot of old dame Griselda Blair, and the punchbowl from which her husband had drunk many a fervent toast to "the king ow're the water;" then there was the queer old chiffonier or bookcase, with its faded volumes of Fielding and Smollet; the dumb waiter; the mirror above the mantelpiece with its painted border, and the old flyblown engravings of the death of Nelson and of Abercrombie, in black and gilded frames.

He was more intent on these objects which spoke so much to him of home and old home memories than on the viands prepared for him by Elsie and Steinie, who bustled about the table, and urged him to sit down and breakfast after his long journey by rail overnight.

"Bodily wants *will* make themselves felt, ye

ken, Mr. Lennard," said Elsie, as she poured out his coffee with one hand and patted his thick brown hair with the other.

In vain he pled that he could not eat, for grief and the rush of thought were choking him.

"But folk can aye drink however deep their grief," she replied, placing the cup before him, with such cream that the spoon might stand in it, fresh eggs and butter, salmon steaks and braxy ham, such as he had never seen since he mounted his desk in the house of Vere, Cheatwood, & Co.

"We couldna' get you a bit of game, even if it were the season, Mr. Lennard," grumbled Steinie; "for in the fields where the partridges used to be thicker than the turnips, and on yon burn-brae where the grouse and ptarmigan blackened the very heather, Mr. Vere, or rather his sporting friends, with twenty guns and mair, breechloaders too, hae made a clean sweep o' everything."

"Never mind the birds or the breakfast," said Lennard, impatiently; "but tell me of my father's ailment. What does the doctor call it?"

"A gradual sinking of the whole system," replied Elsie, who, like Steinie, spoke English, but with a strong Scotch accent, and only an occasional native word. "It is something skill cannot grapple wi' nor care owrecome."

"Old age, Elsie?"

"A broken spirit rather, the minister, Mr. Kirkford, and the doctor say."

Lennard sighed, while Steinic, reckoning on his fingers, said,—

"He would only be sixty come next Beltane day, and I am verging on seventy mysel'."

"Who have been here to see him besides the minister and Dr. Feverley?" asked Lennard.

"Mr. Vere from Blairavon twice, and Miss Vere almost daily for a time; there is well nigh a pack of her calling cards in the silver basket on the chiffonier," replied Elsie.

"But why only for a time?" he asked as a sudden suspicion occurred to him.

"Visitors came; among them a baronet, nae less."

"A baronet?"

"Sir Cullender Crowdy and other great folks. So the small ones at Oakwoodlee were forgotten," continued the old woman spitefully, and without perceiving that her words stung the listener, who had before heard of this distinguished personage, and dreaded Hesbia's flirting propensities; "when she did come it should have been on foot as became her, and not on horseback cutting up the gravel, she and her groom," added Elsie, who bore an especial grudge at the Veres.

We have said, that with a Scottish accent, these old servants spoke pretty pure English, which was lucky, as the broad vernacular of the North, like the dialects of Lancashire or Somersetshire, become boredom to a reader.

The return of Mr. Lennard had been a circumstance which suggested a hundred kind offices, and these two old worthies felt that they could not in any way make too much of him.

"He is fond o' this," said they; "and fond o' that too—a salmon trout from the Dhu-linn," so Steinie fished for it; "new-laid eggs," suggested Elsie; so "this, that, and everything" were alike provided for him, and all his wants, wishes, and comforts affectionately studied. "It is not the key of the street-door in your pocket," says Lever, "nor the lease of the premises in your drawer, that make a *home*. Let us be grateful when we remember that in this attribute the humblest shealing on the hillside is not inferior to the palace of the king."

"We are the last of the auld stock, and must be kind to each other," said Steinie, patting the shoulder of his young master, for he quite identified himself with the family whose bread he had eaten for nearly sixty years—ever since he had been a turnspit in the almost baronial kitchen at Blair-avon.

"But here comes Doctor Feverley," added Steinie.

"I was loth to disturb you, sir, and resolved to wait," said Lennard, rising from an almost untasted breakfast, and presenting his hand, as the Doctor entered; "I have to thank you for the telegram—but—but I hope that you may have over-rated the danger—the urgency."

The Doctor, a pleasant and good-looking young man, apparently not quite thirty years of age, shook his head.

"My dear sir, I fear that I have not exaggerated

the case. For days past your worthy father has been alternately comatose and delirious : these, with the gradual sinking of the pulse for the last thirty-six hours—a hiccough, a pursing of the lips and puffing of the breath, show that the fatal crisis is not far off," said the Doctor sententiously in a whisper.

And a mournful shade fell over Lennard's face on hearing it.

"Oh dear, oh dear!" cried Elsie, covering her face with her apron; "and a' this to be, though I had water brought ilka day frae the Bullion Well of Inchmachan."

"Tush—sulphuretted hydrogen—quite unsuited to the case, my good woman," said the Doctor, with the slightest perceptible irritation, for he had a special animosity to the mineral well referred to. "The patient still sleeps; when he wakes I shall let you see him," added Feverley to Lennard, who sat in a chair, with a crushed heart and a crushed aspect, gazing dreamily at the fields that stretched far away in the distance, dotted by sheep and lambs that lay basking in the morning sunshine.

"I fear that this protracted illness must have intruded on your time, Doctor," he observed after a long pause, on feeling there was a necessity for saying something.

"The social hours and the professional hours of the medical man who does his duty are alike beyond his control," replied Feverley, smiling.

"I have to thank you for unremitting atten-tion—attention and kindness which I can never

repay as they deserve," added Lennard in a broken
voice, as he covered his face with his hands; "but
are you sure that you have not mistaken the signs?"
he asked, clinging still, as it were, to hope.

"Too sure," replied the Doctor, a little emphatically; "compose yourself; the end, thank God, will
be a painless one.   The poor old gentleman is going
fast ' to the far off land and to that city which hath
no need of sun.' "

The Doctor was an anxious, active, and pleasantly-
mannered young man, with a ruddy complexion, a
cheerful, smiling face, sandy-coloured hair, and a well
worn suit of black.   After a hard and thrifty career
of study at the Edinburgh university, he had been
thankful to take the country practice at Blairavon,
with the munificent guaranteed salary of ' forty
pounds per annum for the first year, with a prospect
of being appointed to the parochial board, and
getting such patients as he might pick up under the
patronage of the minister, the family at the mansion-
house, and so forth; but poor Feverley found the
task of "making ends meet" a hard one.   As he
told Lennard at another time, "the blacksmith at
the cross-roads does all the dentistry of the parish,
and the people hereabout are so beastly healthy that
I never have the chance of a good case.   They never
have an ailment; or if they have, a few draughts, to
be had for the drawing, from the mineral well at the
Toxhill, cure all."

"But my father's illness, Doctor: what is it—old
age?"

"Scarcely. It has been as much mental as bodily."

"Mental?"

"More that, perhaps, than the latter. He was always hard pressed for money, as you know; and the worry of a life of conflict with narrow means and its daily routine of debts and duns, have proved rather too much for a proud and haughty temper.

Lennard sighed bitterly, almost angrily, at the doctor's freedom.

"Borrowing cash at ruinous interest from legal harpies, and so on, and so on, till, as you are aware, acre after acre melted away; and now only the house and copsewood of Oakwoodlee remain, of what was once a noble patrimony."

" I am young, Doctor, and the Charter Stone yet is mine," said Lennard, with irritation.

The Doctor gave a feeble little cough, and smiled.

"I have conducted some of his correspondence, and have thus learned that your father has had much to wound his pride during his downward and —pardon me for saying it—improvident career. A Scottish gentleman of the old school— a quaint and often eccentric school, that exists in all ages and countries—he has neither become 'Anglicized on one hand, nor provincialized on the other;' yet he is full of kindly and queer old-fashioned thoughts and sympathies—for instance, his faith in the possession of that ugly block of stone out there, as the palladium of his family."

"My father was always, in the purest sense, a gentleman!" said Lennard, emphatically.

"Undoubtedly; but as for gentlemen," said the Doctor, pursuing some angry thoughts of his own, "in Scotland generally, and in Edinburgh in particular, they have, as some one says somewhere, 'so thinned off of late, or there has been such a deluge of the spurious coin, that one never knows what is real gold;' and nowhere is the spurious brass more current than in all the supposed high places among us."

"But you spoke of my father's ailment as chiefly mental, Doctor," said Lennard, resuming the subject nearest his own heart. "The bitterness of his losses, reverses, and all that, I know; but what more——"

"The discovery of coal on the estate, at the Kaims, after he had parted with it, and the new and unexpected source of great wealth it has become to Mr. Vere, proved the cause of extreme chagrin. He never held up his head after he learned that he had sold, in ignorance of its existence, such a hidden mine of money and relief from all his embarrassments."

"Poor man! poor old man! He had often bored the fields of Kaims, and done so in vain."

"Vere only bored a few inches——"

"Inches!"

"Yes, a few inches deeper in the same places, and found the mineral—a seven-foot seam of pure coal, without the least mixture of clay, and every way equal in quality to the best that the mines of Edinburgh, Glasgow, or Carron can produce."

Lennard bit his nether lip with irrepressible vexation on hearing all this, even though the advantage accrued to the father of Hesbia Vere; and now Elsie Graham, who had slipped away to watch by the sick-bed, came softly in, with her pale and tearful face, to whisper that "the Laird was awake, and asking for Mr. Lennard."

CHAPTER IV.

THE LAST NIGHT ON EARTH.

WITH a heart swollen by many home memories and mournful and tender emotions, Lennard Blair entered the old accustomed room in which, as a little boy, he had been wont to come each morning to receive his father's caress and repeat a prayer.

The oppressive atmosphere of protracted sickness was there now, and an ominous row of phials littered all the mantelpiece. The bed and its faded hangings, the chairs, the table and pictures, the old Indian screen and the oval mirror, all reminded him forcibly of the past; and he sobbed as he hung over his dying father, whose emotions, however, were less violent than he or the Doctor expected.

Around the room were hung pictures of a few favourite racehorses that had once formed part of the Blairavon stud, and, rivalling those of Lord Eglinton, had borne away the bell at Lanark course, the Queen's Plate at Musselburgh, and elsewhere. Some books lay near the bed; one was a Bible, the others were Sir Bernard Burke's compilations and Nisbet's folio on "Heraldry." Lennard knew the old volume well; the ruling passion was strong to the last; but never more would the filmy eyes skim those leaves, to cull out the honours, the quarterings, and the descent of the Blairs of Blairquhan, Blairavon, and that ilk.

The sick man imbibed thirstily some cooling drink, from an old silver tankard which had been filled and emptied at many a jolly hunting breakfast and dinner. It had among its chasings the Blair arms and crest, a stag's head *caboshed*; and had been fashioned from nuggets of the precious metal, found long, long ago, among the green Bathgate hills, when a Stuart filled the Scottish throne, and the Blairs were Lords of Blairavon, fortalice and manor, main and meadow, wood and wold, and cocked their bonnets as high as the Preceptors of St. John or the Lairds of Calder.

Lennard found his father, though wasted and wan to an extent which shocked and distressed him, yet looking so bright in eye and so collected in thought, that he almost hoped yet that young Doctor Feverley might be mistaken; but those very symptoms only convinced the latter that this was the last rally of the senses prior to chaos—to utter extinction.

"My dear, dear boy," said the sufferer, with a quavering voice, "so you have come in time to see me before the starting-bell rings? It *has* rung, Lennard; yet, please God, I shall reach the winning-post. 'There is an hour appointed for all the posterity of Adam,' and mine is coming fast, Lennard," he added, a glance of deep affection mingling in his eyes with that strange, keen, and farseeing expression which is often, if not always, discernible in the eyes of the dying, as if the distant land of Destiny, though all unseen by others, seemed close and nigh to them.

"The bonnie buds have burst in the summer woods, Lennard."

"So I saw, dear father," said the young man, as he seated himself, and retained a clammy hand within his own.

"When the green leaves fall and wither, Lennard, I shall be far, far away, in the Land o' the Leal."

Lennard's tears fell fast.

The likeness between father and son was still striking, though old Richard's hair—that had once been like Lennard's, a rich dark brown—was silvery, thin, and scanty now. His eyes were the same hazel-grey; he had the same straight nose and handsome mouth, though the lips were pursed now and had somewhat fallen in. He gathered a little more strength after Elsie gave him a cup of coffee well dashed with brandy, and with something of a sad smile on his face, he said,—

"Elsie has been a perfect Sister of Mercy to me—hovering noiselessly about my bed, doing a thousand acts of kindness, bestowing blessings, Lennard, and receiving them."

Then he added, more gravely,

"You know what day to-morrow is?"

"The first of May, father."

"An unfortunate—a fatal day for us, as you know, Lennard."

"I cannot believe in such things, father."

"It was on that day my father died of his wounds a week after the battle of Villiers en Couche; at a Beltane time my younger brother Lennard disappeared; on another your poor mother died; on another, nearly my whole estate passed into a stranger's hand; and, by to-morrow, I shall have passed away too!"

"Father," implored Lennard, "do not talk in this way."

"Save that I shall leave you alone—most terribly alone in the world, death is welcome; and, save by yourself and one or two more, I won't be much missed, Lennard," he continued, querulously, and speaking with growing difficulty and at greater intervals; "We old country gentlemen are growing out of fashion; we are behind this 'fast age'—that is the phrase, I believe—and the sooner the last of us is gone the better for those who succeed us. A sea of storms and tempests has the world been to me —a world I leave without regret, but for you, Lennard. God has tried me sorely, and yet, it may be, must be, that I, in many ways, have sorely tempted Him."

Then, as if he remembered that all this morality came rather late after a life of reckless extravagance, he added, in a very broken voice,

"We too often make our own destiny—so have I made mine; and, in doing so, perhaps have blighted

yours. My poor boy, my folly has lost you one of
the finest old estates in the three Lothians, and
were it restored with my health, my folly would
too likely lose it again."

As if the bitterness of thought overwhelmed him,
he closed his eyes and breathed laboriously; then
came the hiccough, that puffing of the lips of which
Feverley had spoken; playing with the bedclothes,
as if the tremulous hands groped in darkness; and
when the eyes opened, they seemed to look vacantly
as if at passing atoms.

At last he spoke again.

"Better it is to be great than rich—better to be
good than either, especially when one comes to lie
where I now am—face to face with eternity. My
boy—my poor boy, would that I knew what Fate
has in store for you after I am gone! Yet, if the
great Book of Destiny were before me, dear Lennard,
I would shrink from turning the page. I can only
pray that there may be, at least, in the future, that
wealth of which I have deprived you."

"My father, do not speak thus; besides, you will
exhaust yourself. Wealth does not ensure happiness. Fear not for me; I am industrious, and shall
work."

"Work!" repeated the old man bitterly, almost
scornfully, as if the word stung him; "there was a
time, but, pshaw! it is past—it is past."

It was not until he had found himself at home, in
that very chamber of sickness, and surrounded by
so many well-remembered features and objects, that

Lennard Blair quite realised—to use a now favourite
and accepted Americanism—that he was face to face
with death, and that his venerated father, the only
link between him and all their storied past, was
actually fading away.

Poor old man! for a time, long as the lives of
most men now in this fast living age of ours, he had
been used to most of the luxuries, and certainly all
the comforts, of the position he had forfeited by
careless improvidence—a position which his son
might never know or enjoy; and now the very
expense of his own funeral harassed him!

It had been an idiosyncrasy of Richard Blair's
character, that while he scorned the imputation of
being obliged to any man, alive or dead, he never
had the slightest hesitation to eke and add to his
miserable fortune by the contraction of debts, the
liquidation of which was a somewhat vague and
hopeless prospect; but a long career of days upon
the turf, of nights at play, of contested elections, of
security for fast friends, and of a hundred other
follies, had rendered such contractions easy and
familiar.

All was well nigh over now; doubts, debts, and
difficulties were at times forgotten, and then he
would imagine himself again the Laird of Blairavon,
and in the great manor house, the turrets of which
overtopped its old ancestral woods.

Tall in figure, though attenuated and thin, he was
a man with a decided presence; the once bronzed face
—bronzed as that of any old Grenadier of the *Garde*

—by exposure in the hunting field, by fishing and
shooting, was pale enough now; the long mustachios were white as snow, and the sunken eyes
were keen and bright, sad and unnaturally beautiful:
and so, while Lennard lingered there, glances were
exchanged full of grief and affection, while they
clasped each others hands, and for spaces of time
remained silent.

It was evident that, without physical pain, the
grim King of Terror was gradually loosing the
"silver cord" of the sufferer, who spoke again, but
this time almost in a whisper.

"I have little to leave you, dear Lennard—oh! so
little, my poor boy; but you'll take care of Elsie if
you can, and old Steinie too; give the poor fellow
my Galloway cob—a welcome gift—he is getting
frail now. Keep what remains of this old place;
and never, while you have life, part with the Charter
Stone; promise me this?"

"I do promise you, father."

"Slender though my means, I ought to have
insured my life for you, Lennard; it was the least
recompense I could have made you for my bad
stewardship."

"Oh, do not talk thus!" entreated Lennard.

"Yes, insured it, that something might accrue to
you—a help, who knows, to regain the old place—
Blairavon I mean, lost—lost by me; but the thought
came too late, and the premium would have ruined
me."

"I am young and strong, father, so think not of me."

"It was my fondest hope, my golden dream, that by your successful efforts, I might one day drive up the old elm avenue that leads to Blairavon gate, its lord and master; but this wild hope can never be realised by me, though by you it may be, Lennard. Oh, it galls me, even in death, the thought that he should be there ———"

"Who, father?"

"That man Vere—the trickster, the money-lender, whose sole knowledge of his family consists in the fact that his father was born before him. But his path has been upward in the world—mine downward; and so the gentleman and the parvenu have changed places."

"Father, father," urged Lennard, somewhat shocked by this pride and bitterness at such a solemn time, "you exhaust and torment yourself."

"I am weak enough—wicked enough it may be, to hate the man for winning what I have lost; and yet—yet, on one account would I forgive him."

"I have no great esteem for him either, father; his manner at times has been both cold and repulsive to me," replied Lennard; "but name the means of your forgiveness—your wish, and I shall tell him."

"Let him marry his absurd-looking daughter— what a shocking seat the girl has on horseback— marry her———"

"To whom?"

"To *you*, and give with her, all the land that once was our own. I have heard your names already jingled together by gossips hereabout."

"For Heaven's sake, dearest father, do not think or talk of such things," said Lennard, glancing hastily round; but fortunately they were quite alone.

Then he became silent, and felt a pang, even in deceiving his father by silence; but little could the proud and querulous old man have understood the honest and true love that was in his son's breast for Hesbia Vere, the daughter of the man he despised, unjustly perhaps; or how nervously Lennard shrunk from the fear that any advance on his part might be coldly repelled, as the trickery of a mere fortune-hunter, following out the path so bluntly and openly recommended.

"However, it is perhaps better that this should not be," added the poor old gentleman, in his anti-quated ideas of the world, of men, and manners.

"Why, father?" asked Lennard, anxiously.

"Because it is by such ill-assorted alliances that the pure *sangre azul*, the blue blood of old families, becomes diluted and spoiled."

Lennard thought otherwise; but he was silent, and full of unhappy and mortifying reflections.

"How much would Mr. Vere value the *sangre azul* of the beggared and bankrupt Blairs of Blairavon?" he pondered, and then reproached himself, as if the question conveyed a censure on his father, who, as the day passed on, sank lower and lower.

"Don't be surprised, Lennard," said Mr. Blair, as if he divined his son's silent thoughts. "My remarks are only the last kick of the old horse—the ruling passion strong in death; greater and weaker men than I, have shown it. As Scott has it, inexorable death 'has closed the long avenue upon loves and friendships, and I look at them as through the grated door of a burial-place filled with the monuments of those who once were dear to me.' Aye, aye; the long avenue of love and friendship is closing now, and growing dark—very dark, indeed, Lennard!"

There were times when his mind wandered, and he seemed to be living over the past again, the years that had gone. Then he would speak of his dead brother as a little playfellow, or he thought of Lennard as a child once more nestling on the knee of his mother, who had long been dead; and then he would mutter of the Charter Stone, of his race-horses and incidents of the betting-ring.

Day passed, and slowly and wearily followed the night of anxiety; the summer sun was gilding brightly the summit of the highest peak of the green Pentland range, the sun of the 1st of May.

"So, so," said Richard Blair, with a smile, as the light seemed to pass out of his eyes, and his clammy grasp of Lennard's hand relaxed; "I have passed my last night on earth, and this Beltane morning I am now going to rejoin her who is not lost, but gone before me—your poor mother who is dead and gone, Lennard—dead and gone!"

He spoke slowly, humbly, and prayerfully of a happier land, and a glorious promise. There was a solemn yet fond farewell on his pinched features, as he turned from the hills that shone in the sunlight, to search for his son's face, and then his spirit passed away.

As the lower jaw fell, and a mortal pallor spread over those beloved features, there rose in the heart of Lennard, a wild desire to clutch at something, to rush away for aid, though all the skill of the College of Physicians would have availed him nothing now !

After he had closed the eyes of the dead, he hung caressingly about the body—*it* was his father, still ; but Dr. Feverley and the parish minister, Doctor Magnus Kirkford, a kind and benevolent old gentleman, unclasped his hands and led him away, leaving Elsie with the body, for she would permit no strange hands to touch it.

If it be true, as some aver, that the eyes of the departed retain upon their filmy retina the likeness of the last person on whom they gazed, then assuredly was the face of Lennard Blair impressed upon the closed orbs of the old man who had just passed away.

"I thought myself a stoic," said poor Lennard, as he seated himself in the sunlit parlour again ; "a stoic," he repeated, for like many other young fellows of his age, he was rather fond of deluding himself into the idea that he was a man of the world, and rather knew what life was ; "but this blow, Doctor

Kirkford, has unmanned me quite, and I feel as if I were a little child again."

"A follower of Zeno at your years, my young friend, you know not what you say ! " replied the old clergyman, patting him kindly on the shoulder. "What would the world come to, if men grew stoics at five-and-twenty ? Yet man is but a shadow, and life a dream. So the old man hath gone to his long home, and his dream of life is over."

"There are times, my dear sir, when I feel my heart like adamant, in a stupor of grief, stolid as Binny Craig; and at others, weak as the water that trickles down its sides."

"All that will pass away anon, my young friend ; for happily God soothes, and Time softens all things."

Reverendly, and with an emotion of compunction, as if he was committing an act of sacrilege, he removed from his dead father's hand an antique signet-ring, with his crest and motto thereon, one which the deceased had always worn. Lennard placed it on a finger, little foreseeing then the part that trinket was to play in the chequered drama of his future life.

CHAPTER V.

BELTANE DAY.

"YOU shall look no more, my young friend! The pinched features which seem to mock life rather than to emulate it, are but an unpleasant memory of a beloved relation; so let the chamber of death be arranged without you."

So spoke kindly but emphatically the Reverend Magnus Kirkford—one of those big, shrewd, warm-hearted, large-brained, and earnest men, with long upper lips, full mental organs, and keen perceptive qualities, who make their mark in the Scottish Church—as he drew Lennard away for the second time from the presence of the dead; then the young man took his hat, left the house, and issued forth into the fields.

The early May morning was beautiful; the sun shone in unclouded brilliance, far away masses of cloud, fleecy-white or cream-coloured, floated over the green wavy slopes of the Pentlands, casting their changing shadows on eminence and ravine, while buried in thought, Lennard strolled slowly on by a deep and grassy path beside a trouting stream,

where aged larches and chestnuts spread their
branches overhead, through which the sunshine fell
in golden flakes and flashes on the reeds and water-
lilies that floated on the current, and on an occasional
brown trout, as it shot with the speed of light over
"the unnumbered pebbles." Amid the solitude
there was no sound but the gurgle of the water, and
the hum of the mountain bee as it buried itself in
the drooping cups of the pink foxglove or the Scottish
bluebell.

The place was conducive to thought and to
melancholy. Lennard's old trouting stream was
flowing then as it had flowed when he, a child, had
launched fleets of walnut-shells upon its bosom —
unchanging, unceasing, never fading, shrinking, or
growing older—and he gazed on its gurgling current as on the face of an early friend.

The rattle of a train of heavily-laden carts passing
along the distant highway from Vere's coal-pits at
the Mains of Kaims, was a novel sound there;
but whichever way Lennard turned, some old and
familiar object inseparably connected with the past,
with the dead, or with his happy, heedless boyhood,
met his eye.

In an adjacent meadow his father's old Galloway
cob—one of those sturdy little horses alleged by the
Galwegians to have sprung from the stallions of
the wrecked Spanish armada—was quietly grazing.
Here were trees and yonder hedges of his own
planting. Two miles distant some light-grey smoke
curled up from amid the green woodlands, and he

knew that there stood the stately old mansion of
Blairavon.

Nearer on the sunny hill-slope was the less pre-
tentious house of Oakwoodlee, with all the window-
blinds drawn closely down, according to the Scottish
custom at such a solemn time; thus by its aspect
seeming so indicative of silence, of desolation, of
death, and of the presence of one who would never
cross its threshold save once again, borne slowly
shoulder high.

Yonder was the Charter Stone, round which so
many local and family legends hovered. The great
block of ages past, where his ancestors and King
James IV. had hobbed and nobbed at a hunting-
party, in the days when fords were scarce and
waters deep, and when bulls and stags were thick as
wild berries in the woods of Blairavon and Calder;
and further off, at the base of Craigellon—an eminence of grey rock, tufted with yellow broom, lay
the pond, the lochlet or rushy tarn, in which, on a
Beltane day, some thirty years ago, his uncle
Lennard had been found drowned.

Could it really be true that Beltane, the 1st of
May, was a day of destiny to his family? Did such
an idea not seem absurd in these our days of steam
and telegraphy, of mental power, of progress, and of
paper collars?

Till informed by Elsie Grahame and Stephen
Hislop, Lennard never knew the exact story of his
uncle's fate; for something of sorrow and mystery

in it had always sealed his father's lips on the subject.

It would seem that before the marriage of Lennard's mother, Richard Blair and his brother had both loved her; but she preferred the elder, so the younger disappeared on the day subsequent to the wedding, Beltane morning, greatly to the grief and dismay of all the family.

In vain was the country searched, and in vain were the innkeepers and ostlers on every route and line of road examined. There were no railways in Scotland then, so the guards and drivers of the mails were questioned, and the church-doors of all the adjacent parishes placarded. In vain were advertisements inserted in the public prints, for no trace was found of the lost man till the exact day twelvemonths after his disappearance, when Steinie Hislop's otter terrier discovered a dead body, —sorely decomposed, disfigured, and almost reduced to a skeleton—among the reeds and broad-leaved water-docks, in the little loch under Craigellon.

From various indications, but chiefly the remains of his dress, it was declared to be the body of Lennard Blair; but whether in his grief and mortification he had committed suicide, whether he had fallen into the loch by accident, or been assaulted and flung in, no one could assume with certainty. The circumstance that neither ring, purse, nor watch were found upon him seemed to indicate some dark tragedy, more especially as gypsies had been seen in the woods about the time of his dis-appearance; but it was a case of which neither the sheriff nor the procurator-fiscal for the county could make anything. So the remains were laid in the grave of the Blairs, in the old and secluded churchyard of Inchmachan, and the story, a "nine-days' wonder" while it lasted, was speedily committed to oblivion by all save Richard Blair, who sincerely loved his brother, and long mourned in secret his untimely fate.

From gazing at Craigellon and reflecting on this dark story, Lennard turned thoughtfully to that other landmark of his family, the great monolith called the Charter Stone; the retention of which was alleged by tradition to be so inseparably connected with the fortune of the Blairs, that it had actually occupied the dying thoughts of his father.

Without being vulgarly superstitious—though to give undue weight to idle fancies is often the peculiarity of the German and the Scot—Lennard was too much of the latter to be able to thrust aside the old and inbred feeling. Though no believer in spiritualism, or other semi-extinct absurdities, he thought that there might be a world unseen by and unknown to us; a world, of which we have lost the key, or never possessed it. He thought that nature might have her night-side, as Mrs. Crowe has laboured hard to shew us, and that there may be "more things in heaven and earth," than Horatio dreamt of in his philosophy.

A standing stone of the Druid days, it had probably been there ages before the Romans had their flying camp on the mains of Kaims, and was covered now by masses of green moss and russet-coloured lichens.

It was a strange coincidence, that on the day before his disappearance, his uncle Lennard, when probably wandering there in sadness and bitterness of heart, had carved his name on the monolith, in some freak, or lest he should too soon be forgotten, perhaps.

Such solid symbols of the possession of land as this Charter Stone are not uncommon in Scotland.

They were often used to denote a right to the soil long before written documents became general, and frequently had—like the Pillar of Refuge, at Torphichen—ideal privileges attached to them. If a man set his back against the monolith of this description in Girvan, he supposed himself able to defy the law of arrest; nor could cattle fastened thereto be poinded for debt. Such, perhaps, was the Charter Stone of old Dailly in Carrick, which the people, a few years ago, would not permit to be removed, lest misfortune should fall upon the locality. Such was the stone of the Glove at *Clach-mannan;* such, no doubt, was the famous old Blue Stone, some twenty feet long, now buried in the Castle Hill of Edinburgh; the Clach-na-Cudden of Inverness, and such was literally the Chair of Fate at Scone, the charter stone of the kingdom. So the story of the Charter Stone of the Blairs was simply an old Scottish idea, and not a solitary one either.

There was an angry blush on Lennard's cheek as
he thought of how his practical, hard-working, everyday friends in Liverpool would have laughed at the
dreams in which he was indulging, for he had now
gone back, as we have said, to the pastoral, lonely,
and narrow world from which he had emerged under
the patronage of Mr. Vere; but from his reverie he
was roused by a sound, and on the highway at the
base of the slope on which the great stone stands,
there dashed past an elegant mail-phæton, a very
"fast" looking affair, with patent lever break and
plated axles, drawn by a pair of spanking geldings
fifteen hands high.

A lady was seated beside the gentleman who drove
them, and Lennard felt his pulses quicken as they
swept along with wheels and harness flashing in the
sun. They were chatting and laughing, even loudly,
together; in one he recognized Hesbin Vere, and in
the other, beyond a doubt, his impertinent fellow-
traveller by the express train; and now, deep
though his present grief, some very unpleasant and
conflicting thoughts occurred to him.

He looked at his watch: the hour was early—
barely ten in the forenoon—so whither could they
be bound? To some pic-nic, steeplechase, otter-
hunt, or other scene of thoughtless happiness, no
doubt, while he——he turned in bitterness away.

A great grief makes us selfish sometimes; even
so does a great love; so in the midst of his sharp
sorrow Lennard Blair had almost forgotten the exis-

tence of Hesbia Vere since the moment his father
had spoken of her.

Amid that sorrow worldly thoughts *would* intrude
themselves, for he knew that even the wreck of
his father's fortune was embarrassed, and thus,
that his own monetary future was uncertain and
shadowy.

Lennard freely spoke of these fears to Doctor
Feverley, a kind and good-hearted fellow, who now
spent much of his leisure time with him, for he pitied
the loneliness of young Blair, who had now not a
near relation in the world.

Cards " of condolence," glazed and embossed, per
powdered and plushed footmen, came promptly
enough from Blairavon and from the houses of old
country friends, who remembered Richard Blair
when he was the Master of the Foxhounds and
hunted the county as it had never been hunted
since, and when he was the king of good fellows,
with his cellars and stables full; but Lennard took
their " bits of pasteboard " for as much as they
were worth, and clung thankfully and gratefully to
the companionship of the young Doctor.

The mode of half-intimacy and half-patronage
in which he was received at Blairavon and some of
the other great mansions in the neighbourhood—he,
a scholar, a gentleman by education, by conduct,
and by diploma—had stung Frank Feverley to the
quick at first; but he had an aged mother to sup-
port,—a mother who doted on him, and who con-

ceived him to be the greatest light in the school of
medicine, one to whom Simpson, Bell, and Hunter
were as nothing; so the Doctor consoled himself by the old Scottish proverb, " he yat tholis
overcomes," and thus, for her sake, was the con-
queror in the end.

After the mockery of dining that day, as they
lingered over a bottle of fine old Madeira which
Steinie had carefully aired in the sunshine, the
Doctor strove to encourage Lennard by his advice.

" Your good father, Mr. Blair, fought the battle
of life sturdily, if not wisely, and now ' after life's
fitful fever he sleeps well.'   But you will agree with
me, that it is futile to be regretfully looking into
the past as he did; for the past can return no
more."

" True, Doctor, true—it has ceased to be ours."

" So our task should be to improve the *present*,
and to hope for all in the future."

" And such shall be my course, Feverley."

" I am glad to hear you say so, for such has been
mine, and I have seldom known the system to fail."

" My two or three thousands are, I know, but a
trifle in the great capital of Vere, Cheatwood, and
Co., but still I am useful, especially with their
Spanish and South American correspondence.   I
work hard—at times I literally drudge like a slave
—and may well hope to treble and quadruple my
little sum in time.   Then I have still this old jointure-house and the land of Oakwoodlee, or a fragment

of it; after the—the funeral we shall know all," he added with a quivering lip.

For us, says a brilliant female writer, "mercifully the capacity of suffering is blunted as the years go by; the mental nerves lose their sensitiveness; the mind, like the body, grows hard; and the agony of to-day will become the passing annoyance of twelve months hence."

Though mortifications, jealousies, bitterness, and slights incident to his subordinate position and slender means were nothing new to Lennard Blair, whose naturally generous and fiery spirit they chafed and exasperated, sorrow was a novel suffering, and he felt that the death of his old father was indeed a keen, keen *wrench*.

But one more scene remained to act out the domestic tragedy before he could leave Oakwoodlee— the funeral day,—and it came in due time.

CHAPTER VI.

DUST TO DUST.

AMONG the various cards that littered the table, Lennard looked in vain for one of Hesbia Vere.

"This may be an oversight, or it may be that she deems her father's message sufficient," thought he, and thus strove to allay the gnawing doubt that was in his heart.

The day of the funeral came, and for long after it had passed away did the whole scene float like a dream in Lennard's memory. The bright sunshine, the green summer woods, the gathering friends, the tread of many feet where all had been silence before, the bustle of carriages; the gloomy hearse, with its mocking plumes, under which lay the last real friend he had on earth; the mattocks and shovels; and by the old grey churchyard-wall, the deep grave, that lay "lurking and gaping for its prey!"

The whole affairs of the day seemed a species of phantasmagoria, amid which Lennard acted and moved like an automaton. His situation was, to him, a novel one; and he was watched by a few sympathizing, and by many curious eyes, for he was the last of an old and long-respected family.

Richard Blair's inordinate pride of the latter, his old-fashioned estimate of the fortuitous claims of birth, which jarred so oddly with his poverty, were all forgotten now; and those who had often laughed at him therefor, as they gathered in the antique and plainly furnished dining-room, to partake of a little luncheon before " the lifting," as it is locally phrased, looked up with real respect and melancholy interest to the portraits of the Blairs of other times—full-lengths from Blairavon, a world too large for Oakwoodlee—stately fellows in wigs and long waistcoats or cuirasses, who had fought for the Stuarts at Killycrankie, Dunkeld, and Dunblane; and powdered dames, whose patches, rouge, and smiles had vanquished the heroes of Falkirk and Fontenoy, of Minden and Quebec.

How intensely Lennard wished the whole affair over !

There was the darkened or subdued light in the apartment; the groups of half-strangers, who whispered of the weather, crops, and cattle, or sat moodily silent; the cold greetings and formal grasping of hands; the solemn faces made up for the occasion; the greedy fellows in corners enjoying the cold beef and wine or the cakes and whisky!

Then the absence of nearly all religious ceremonial seemed irreverent to the dead, and shocking to Lennard, accustomed as he had been for some years past to the service of the Church of England, to

strange and ritualistic forms, and to prayers intoned
by surpliced clergymen in red-lined Oxford hoods.
Yet poor old Doctor Magnus Kirkford's extempore
invocation came straight from his earnest and honest
heart, though it might have sounded painfully harsh,
and perhaps vulgar, in the ear of a dainty Oxonian
Lutheran, who may lisp his devotions with the aid
of a diamond ring, a cambric handkerchief, and
parted hair.

Close by the minister stood the portly person of
Mr. John Vere (in his own estimation the first man
in the parish), musing, and playing with large handfuls of loose silver, a custom he had when plunging
his hands deep into his trowsers-pockets, for Vere
was never known to have a purse.

The prayer of the Calvinist was followed by
a chapter from Isaiah, a new and excellent feature
amid the almost barbarous plainness that marks the
Scottish funeral; and then the train of carriages
wended slowly through the shady lanes and summer
woods towards the old parish church.   Mr. Vere
was, of course, in his own showy vehicle; it brought
up the rear of the funeral train, which was accom-
panied by many of the old tenantry afoot, and each
and all were clad in that clean and sober black-cloth
suit which few of the Scottish peasantry, however
poor or humble, are without.

Among his neighbours of former times, Richard
Blair had been deemed a fine jolly fellow, a boon
companion over a bottle of Burgundy or whisky-
toddy, a good rider across the stiffest hunting

country, never was known to "funk" at a double
ditch or a stone wall, and as one who always rode
straight to hounds. Many of those old neighbours
of the hunt were dead and gone, and among their
sons he had been viewed simply as a bore—a proud,
soured, cynical, and morbidly discontented old man;
while Lennard, though not blind to his father's
defects of temper and former failings, could view
him now only through the softening medium of grief
and filial regard.

"Poor old Blairavon!" he heard Ranald Cheyne
of the Haughs—a fine old ruddy-faced country gentleman—say to another, as they dismounted at the
churchyard-gate; "he used to be a two-bottle man
in my day, and the king of all good fellows!"

"Hush, Mr. Cheyne! that is his son," said Doctor
Feverley, who was near.

"Little Lennard—I remember, I remember him
now," replied the other, as he shook Lennard's hand
kindly, and pressed him to come over and see him
and his girls at the Haughs, where a knife and fork
would always be ready for him; but Lennard answered vaguely, for he was in a land of painful
dreams.

"Good Heaven! how the time passes," resumed
Mr. Cheyne; "it seems but yesterday when we had
that slapping run with the Linlithgow foxhounds at
Boghall, when only three riders out of a large field
were in at the death—your worthy father, Mr.
Lennard, old Hislop, and myself. Poor Steinie! he
is, I see, sorely cut up," added Ranald Cheyne, who,

though the head of one of the best county families,
kindly shook the hand of the old servant.

Several other foxhunting friends were there volun-
tarily, for they still remembered the jolly fellow of
other times, and recognized in the dead Laird of
Blairavon a person of consideration and distinction,
and their sturdy champion against Parliamentary
Reform and the Corn-law League.

The ancient church, dedicated to a holy man
of the olden time—the Scottish Saint Machan,
who died in the 9th century—crowns a steep and
grassy knoll, at the base of which flows a brawling stream. Thick old copsewood, amid which the
white walls of the pretty manse are peeping, sur-
rounds the knoll, which is studded with old
headstones half sunk in the long rank grass that
sprouts above the dust of many, many generations.

Ruined at the storm of the Reformation, and
repaired amid the stern wars of the Covenant, the
old stained glass of its arched windows has long
since given place to square panes of green-bottle
hue, with bulls'-eyes in the centre of many; but the
deep doors of the Scoto-Norman period, with their
zig-zag mouldings and grotesque carvings still remain
unchanged as when the Crusaders of St. John had
their banner floating on Torphichen, and Scotland's
kings held royal state in their noblest palace at
Linlithgow.

The vault of the Blairs had always been on the
south side. This aisle, or side of every ancient
church, had the pre-eminence in memory of an old

tradition, that when our Saviour died he had turned towards the south; so, in great churches, there stood the abbot's chair, and there most persons of rank were buried.

As the funeral train, all on foot now, passed into the burying-ground, a young man who stood on the slope by which the gate is approached, and who seemed to be loitering there out of mere curiosity, lifted his wide-awake hat and stood uncovered.

As this token of respect to the passing dead is little known in the lowlands of Scotland—or has been so since the Reformation—Lennard regarded the stranger with some interest, and recognized the saucy face, the fair mustachios, and goatee-beard of his railway companion.

What secret emotion was it that made him, even in that solemn time of grief, shrink from this man's cold, enquiring and impudent eyes—eyes in which he read, somehow, the expression of enmity and future mischief, for over the face of the loiterer there spread something of a sneering smile, as he replaced his hat and turned away with his fishing-rod.

Before the dark procession, shovel on shoulder, marched old Malcolm Mattox, the grave-digger. Even he was sad, and soberly clad in a venerable and rusty suit of black; and thus he led the way to the ground where the Blairs lie, "whar he had ne'er made a lair," as he whispered to Steinie, since Lennard's mother had been laid beside that unfortunate brother, who had not loved her "wisely, but too well."

I.   F

The summer wind rustled the green leaves of the
old woods with a sighing sound, that mingled with
the sobs of a few aged people, who thought of all
the past, and sorrowed for the kind and passionate,
but ruined old gentleman; and those sighs of the
wind and sobs of the people seemed, somehow, to
speak to young Lennard's grateful heart of the rest
his dead father had found.

At last it was all over; Mattox's shovel had batted
down the last sod, and he had touched his bonnet
and withdrawn. Friends and followers were gone,
and with a pressure of the hand, and a general invitation to Lennard to "turn up at Blairavon," Mr.
Vere went towards his carriage.

"Come over," continued Hesbia's portly papa,
"whenever you feel up to the mark—that is, tired
of your own company, or a longing for ours."

"Thanks —— "

"We've always a knife and fork—a spare cover
or two laid, you can never be in the way. Remember, luncheon at 2, dinner at 7—our old time for
both, as out at our villa on the Aigburth Road. But
my advice to you would be, to get back to your desk;
nothing is so soothing to the nervous system as
business;" and, jingling the handfuls of silver that
lurked in the depths of his right pocket, he retired.

Lennard found himself again in the lonely parlour
of Oakwoodlee, with Elsie Graham hovering near
him.

His father's old and well-worn arm-chair was
opposite: he did not occupy it, but preferred to sit

and fancy the outline of the old man in it, and think that something of his presence still hovered there. His silver-headed cane was in the chimney-corner close by, and under the chair were still his slippers and his favourite old otter terrier.

For reasons of his own, Lennard Blair was in no haste to return to Liverpool; he passed several days alone, seeing nothing even of Feverley, nothing of his friends at Blairavon, and hearing of Hesbia only that which he had rather was not told him.

Lennard found, as he had expected, that save the house and its furniture, the old family pictures and mementos, with the little piece of coppice, the shooting thereof, and the right of fishing in the adjacent stream, nothing remained to him; that there were many debts to pay, and that now more than ever must his chief dependence be on his desk in the house of Vere, Cheatwood and Co. But he experienced somewhat of a shock, together with a glow of gratitude, when he spoke of the future of his two old dependents.

"You have saved something, I hope, Steinie?" said he anxiously, to old Hislop.

"Saved, Mr. Lennard?" repeated Steinie, confusedly.

"You have been so long with my father, Steinie —you, and Elsie too."

"Oh yes, Mr. Lennard," answered Elsie, curtseying and answering for both; "Steinie and I have both saved and laid bye for a rainy day; but alack! it has proved one of wintry storm to us."

"I am so glad of your thrift; those savings will help you now."

"No muckle, Mr. Lennard, I fear," sighed Steinie, as the colour deepened on his old and withered face.

"Steinie!" ejaculated Elsie, in a tone of reprehension.

And now, after a time, and much circumlocution, Lennard learned that, during his father's protracted illness or decline, these two faithful old creatures had spent all their little hoardings in procuring for him much that he would have been unable to obtain for himself; and that he had passed away in ignorance of where the money came from! So Lennard resolved that, in future, Oakwoodlee should be, as it had hitherto been, their home, with such an allowance as he could spare them out of his pittance at Liverpool.

Fierce and stubborn had been the long struggle between the old pride of the Blairs and their new poverty, ere Richard, whilom of Blairavon, would permit his son, with the money he inherited from his mother, to engage in mercantile pursuits under the auspices of the more wise and thrifty speculator who won the acres which he, himself, had not the sense to keep; but, luckily, Lennard liked business, and prudently had been most attentive thereto; viewing it, perhaps, as the beginning of an end—as the means to an ultimate consummation.

Yet now, when again in his native scenes,—when, after the weariness of incessant work, the ceaseless

grinding, the hurlyburly, din and rush of life in
Liverpool, by street and dock, by road and river, he
felt how grateful indeed was the calm of Oakwoodlee, and the pure breeze that came from the
great slopes of the Pentland Hills, laden with the
fragrance of the purple heather and the golden bells
of the gorse bushes, while the scenery around the
old house, the older church of King David's days,
the trouting burn, and the quaint bridge that
spanned it, filled his heart with soft and gentle
emotions.

The yellow broom, the hawthorn pink and white,
the gorgeous laburnum and purple lilac, the gueldre
rose, with its snow-white bells and tender green
leaves, were in all their beauty now; while the
violet with its sweet perfume, the pansy with its
velvet leaves, the lily and tulip, were duly developed
under Steinie's care in the little garden.

Old Elsie had one great weakness of character.

Displaced from what she conceived to be her high
estate as housekeeper at Blairavon, she loathed the
lucky Veres as veritable intruders, as if they had
won the place by the sword, by fraud or force, instead of in the open market; and poor Miss Vere
came in for her share of especial dislike.

"As for that madam, Miss Hesbia," said she, a
few days after the funeral, when Lennard was
smoking moodily at the parlour window; "she'll
never come to any but an ill end."

"Of whom are you permitting yourself to talk so
freely, Elsie?"

"As the poor laird that's dead and gone used to call her, the proud parvenoo's daughter, which means, I suppose, something that's dishonest."

"How—why, what on earth do you mean, Elsie?" asked Lennard with undisguised asperity in his tone. "Do you refer to Miss Vere?"

"To who else, Mr. Lennard! To see her in kirk, either here or at Inchmachan, flaunting her ribbons and laces, smoothing her hair, fitting and refitting her dainty kid gloves, and jangling her bracelets. And then she whispers, and leers, and laughs so with that gentleman——"

"Which gentleman—who?" asked Lennard with forced indifference of manner, thinking of him of the mail-phaeton and white wide-awake.

"Oh any one—any one, a' are welcome fish that come into her net."

Aware as he was of Hesbia's flirting proclivities, the remark stung Lennard deeply.

"And on the Sabbath," resumed Elsie. "My only wonder is——"

"Is what?"

"That nae judgment has yet fallen upon her; but her pride will have a fall, sae sure as my name is Elsie Graham!"

"Do not talk nonsense, or be so uncharitable, Elsie; and leave me just now, as I would rather be alone," replied Lennard, unwilling that this sharp-sighted old woman should detect perhaps his secret thoughts, which were far from pleasant ones, for she had mentioned incidentally more than once that

Miss Vere had been seen riding, driving, sketching, and rambling about "mair than was beseeming," with a gentleman who was on a visit to her father.

He knew her weakness, her vanity—great almost as her beauty; and jealousy, with anger, grew strong within him, for in his frame of mind, weakened by recent sorrow and thus easily impressionable, suspicions soon became convictions, as his heart began to exchange its grief for bitterness.

"I shall take Vere's advice, and start for Liverpool to-morrow—plunge again into the whirl of business, of dissipation perhaps, and forget all about her! I must push on somehow," he would say to himself; "I must make more rapid steps towards my El Dorado—towards fortune. I cannot be a subordinate, a quill-driving clerk, for ever, like poor old Envoyse and thousands of others, who have let slip that chance which every man has at least *once* in life. So Liverpool be it again!".

And yet he lingered on at the lonely and almost voiceless house of Oakwoodlee, in the hope of seeing Hesbia Vere, though the complications of his position with her father made his love for her a matter of difficulty to develop or declare, much more so than if she had been the daughter of any other man, even with all their great disparity of means and prospects for the future; and yet he could not deny himself the half-desperate hope, the pleasing flattery, of creating for himself some lasting and permanent interest in her heart ere it might be lost to him for ever.

CHAPTER VII.

DAY DREAMS.

SLOWLY passed the days while he lingered at home, where the change was a great and complete one, away from the bustle of Liverpool, with its theatres, concerts and flower-shows, regattas and balls, the rush of cabs and carriages, the rattle of omnibuses and lumbering vans or laden lorries; away from its miles of docks and mighty fleets of merchantmen; away from protested bills, discount and interest, legitimate acceptances, custom-house clearances, ledger and daybook, bills of lading, charter-parties, telegrams, letters and files, invoices and inventories, and all the bother and slang of business, which are as Sanscrit or Oordoo to the upper ten thousand of her Majesty's lieges.

Away from the dingy counting-room in that narrow alley off Canning Place; away from the crowded quays, the taverns, back parlours, tea-gardens, and billiard-rooms; away from Sundays on the river and trips to Birkenhead; away from cosy dens, where quiet little dinners were had, and where clerks and confidentials like old Mr. Envoyse took the air and drank their beer or Cape Madeira, and compared notes of firms and failures, while pressing the tobacco into their pipes or rolling up their cigarettes, with knowing glances and eyes half-closed the while.

Lennard was away from all this now, and back once more to the green, sequestered world of his boyhood.

The great house at Blairavon, he had been told, was full of visitors, scarcely one of whom he had seen as yet; but he heard frequently of Hesbia, whose name was mixed up with that of a certain mysterious baronet, who rejoiced in the odd patronymic of Sir Cullender Crowdy. The fear of rivalry grew strong in his heart; and as he brooded over what was now, together with all that *might* have been—the past, the present, and the future—he felt for the time no very good feeling towards the great world that lay beyond the windows of Oakwoodlee.

He remembered that Miss Vere had called frequently there—almost daily—during his father's last illness.

Why did she abstain from coming now? To be sure, there was no lady to visit; but Hesbia despised all prudery, and was not wont to stand greatly on trifles or punctilio either.

Days passed, during which he never ventured near Blairavon; an uncertain emotion of half doubt, half childish pique at Miss Vere, withheld him.

Inspired by his father's teaching, Lennard Blair,

though by no means a visionary, but rather a practical and hard-working fellow, had more than once, when standing under the stately old trees, the leaves of which had fallen on generations of his ancestors, looked with intense regret at the old mansion of Blairavon, at the fair estate of fertile field and grassy meadow, hamlet and hedgerow, stretching away to the hills, so rich and beautiful in aspect— he looked, we say, but sadly and wistfully, for never would it be his, as it had been his sires' in the days of old !

It was gone, irrevocably gone, by no fault of his; and as he turned away, a vague, unuttered vow would rise to his lips.

Dreams—golden ones certainly—of more active means of attaining his ultimate hope, and of his father's desire, would come upon him, as he lay stretched on the green sward, gazing into the depths of the blue sky, while the old rooks cawed monotonously in the great gnarled trees close by.

Of how many adventurers had he heard who, in the fertile wastes of Australia, by the Swan River, the land of kangaroo-skins, of the vine, and the olive, or in some remote isle of the Pacific or Southern Sea, discovered their "El Dorado," where gold and gems and treasure were amassed as in an Arabian tale ?

True; but, suggested Prudence, of how many, many *more*, who strive only to fail and die, do we hear nothing? Courage, energy, perseverance, and bodily strength were required for such a vague and hard career. All these he had; but there was Hesbia—the light round which he had fluttered like a moth—could he relinquish the chance, the slender chance, of winning her love, or at least of relieving his heart by the declaration of his own?

The progress to fortune, at his desk in the dark alley off Canning Place, would be a slow one.

"Oh, the heartless weariness of working eternally for other people, and never for one's self!" he exclaimed bitterly, as he struck his hands together.

Yet it was there, in that dingy Liverpool alley, he had garnered up his hopes of realizing an independence—of winning—dared he hope she would wait for him?—Hesbia Vere. He had always pictured a visionary ideal, as few young men have not, of what the woman he would love ought to be; and *now* he thought that he had found this ideal realised in her.

"But how am I ever to propose to this proud and coquettish girl," thought he, "with my monetary recommendations—my paltry share in the firm, my small salary, and the acre or two round the old Jointure House? With much of hope, but no certainty in the future, could I go to that most mercenary fellow, old Vere, and ask for his only daughter and heiress?"

Then his father's somewhat selfish words occurred to him: "Let him marry his absurd-looking daughter to you, and give with her all the land that was once our own,"—and he shivered at the recollection of how they sounded, and at the thought of how his passion might be viewed by Hesbia as well as by her father; and he nervously shrunk from the double chance of rejection and ridicule.

"Her regard for me, if she has such, or her toleration of my attention, may be a whim, and a whim only; but, with all her father's regard for her, how would he view even that passing fancy?"

And Lennard smiled bitterly to himself.

He heard a light step—a shadow fell across him, and he found two bright and beautiful eyes bent with a quizzical expression on his own, as a tall and very handsome girl stood beside him, with the bird-of-paradise plume in her smart hat dancing in the wind, while she twirled with a rapid little hand the parasol that rested on her plump and rounded shoulder.

A large and showy girl, with a creamy complexion and rich colour, a nose *retroussé* in the slightest degree, bright brown eyes and soft brown hair, full red lips that were rather large, perhaps, and a general complexion and expression of great brilliance; she was Hesbia Vere, dressed in a most becoming summer-suit of plain Holland linen, trimmed with blue braid; but her gloves, boots, collar, brooch, and earrings were all in admirable taste.

"Miss Vere!" exclaimed Lennard, as he sprang to his feet; "I beg pardon for not seeing you approach."

"Or hearing me either," said she; "I have been watching you for the last half-hour."

"Impossible!"

"For ten minutes—two at least. Are you composing poetry, or what?"

"Poetry!—no—but why?"

"You were muttering and talking to yourself."

"I have no one else to talk to."

"And whose fault, sir, is that pray?"

"My own perhaps, Hesbia."

"Miss Vere, say, please; we cannot play at flirtation and laughing love-making among you sobersided Scotch folks, as we may do at home."

"Play at love-making!" repeated Lennard, with mingled sadness and annoyance; "it would soon be playing with fire, if one attempted it with you."

"Oh, don't try to flatter me, please, or I may get up a beautiful blush."

"You have been too much occupied ever to think of me, poor lonely wretch, in the old house yonder," said he, offended by the levity of her bearing.

"Occupied, Mr. Blair! with what, or with whom do you mean?"

"Visitors — one visitor in particular, by all accounts."

"I am watched, then, it seems, though I am accountable for my conduct to no one but papa. But now, don't become disagreeable," she added, with one of her brightest and most tender smiles, as she took his arm uninvited; "come with me for a little walk, and I shall tell you why I actually was about to visit Oakwoodlee."

"You were coming to visit me, Hesbia?"

"No, Lennard — but, for the future, remember that I am Miss Vere, and you Mr. Blair — I was going but to leave my own note in passing—this, an invitation for you to dine with us on the day after to-morrow, at six o'clock—you'll come, of course."

"With pleasure," said Lennard; and then he added, gloomily, "I suppose I must."

"Must? Oh, fie! jealous again—poor Lennard —I beg pardon, Mr. Blair I mean; why, the gentleman you are thinking of is only my cousin."

"Your cousin a baronet?"

"A baronet—my cousin Travice; Mr. Blair, what are you talking about?" she asked, with a flush of irritation; but don't be so jealous, I implore you," she added, with one of her sweet waggish smiles.

"Oh, Hesbia, that I had the right to be!"

"Men can be jealous whether they have the right or not."

"There can be no jealousy without love," said the young man in a tremulous voice, and in a manner there could be no mistaking.

"You are in error," said Miss Vere, parrying the speech, or unheeding its inference; "jealousy may exist with perfect hatred. My cousin and I are together in a dull country-house; he compliments my singing, which you have often told me was excellent; he praises my seat on horseback, which you have admitted was admirable; he finds

it heavy work swaying me into the saddle, which,
I think you have discovered also,—but he adjusts
my foot so nicely in the stirrup! He pays me all
sorts of attention, just as you, Sir Cullender Crowdy,
and a hundred others have done and may do, and
yet don't mean anything. I take them for what
they are worth; and every pretty girl—you too
have admitted that I am pretty, Lennard—does
precisely the same."

Lennard sighed, borne away by her rattling
manner, and bewildered by the strange charm of
her presence and her brilliant beauty, he pressed
against his side the hand that rested on his arm, and
half thought the pressure was returned upon it; but
Hesbia was too subtle in her coquetry to do a very
decided thing.

At intervals Lennard had heard of this cousin
Travice Cheatwood, but never for good, and always
for evil and mischief. He had heard of Hesbia being
frequently with him at public places in Liverpool,
but singularly enough, he and Travice had never
met. He afterwards found, that when he had received certain hints of engagements, or more plainly
that he was *not* to visit Mr. Vere's villa near Aigburth,
on particular evenings, they were invariably the
occasion on which "Cousin Travice" was expected!

The memory of those suspicions came back to
Lennard's mind unpleasantly now.

Latterly, for some extravagance in his career at
college, Travice Cheatwood had been completely
banished from his uncle's family cricle, so that it was

a source of extreme annoyance to Lennard, his being
domiciled at Blairavon now.

"Still pouting, Mr. Blair?   Well, I shall call you
Lennard, if by so doing I can smooth your wrinkled
front.   Let us be as good friends here as we usually
are at Liverpool, for there I always find you charming.   I am wilful, naughty, tiresome——"

"Hesbia!"

"Yes, tiresome at times; but you will find me
charming, too, for all that; and like myself, you have
rather an aptitude for fun and flirting."

"I am in no mood for fun."

"Of course not, just now, my poor friend."

"And as for flirting, you are the last girl in
the world with whom I would ever think of doing
so."

"The last—I—why?" she asked, with real surprise and inquiry in her clear, deep hazel eyes.

His voice trembled as he spoke, and the colour
deepened in the cheek of Miss Vere, while gratified
vanity flashed in her eyes; then her heavy lids
drooped, and she said, with a merry laugh,

"I shall not seek to lure you into danger; so
come, don't let us grow serious, for you know how I
detest serious people; and in the country for you
and I to become so would be equally unbearable and
absurd."

Lennard sighed with real annoyance at the
hopeless or studied frivolity of her manner, as they
walked slowly onward through a shady and grassy
lane.

There are some persons in the world who are said to love whoever, or rather whatever, they pity. Hesbia for the time was one of these, and in reality at that moment—though an egregious flirt—she felt that she actually loved the sad-eyed and lonely Lennard Blair of that broken home, that desolate old house at Oakwoodlee; but she would have shrunk nervously from affording him the slightest inkling as to this temporary state of her thoughts.

CHAPTER VIII.

HESBIA VERE.

THE beauty of Hesbia Vere was certainly great and striking; but though perfectly English in its character, dangerous in its quality, sparkling and brilliant, it was not aristocratic. She had a remarkable bearing; but it was the confidence derived from a consummate knowledge of the possession of that beauty and the admiration it excited, combined with wealth and utter freedom of thought and action.

The county dames declared that Miss Vere was not ladylike, yet admitted her attractions, while the gentlemen averred that she was decidedly a "stylish girl," and that phrase expressed all.

She had a singular fascination in the brightness of her smile, in the modulation of her voice, and in all her ways, particularly in a charming playfulness of manner; yet she was in heart and soul a coquette. A year or so younger than Lennard Blair, she was more than ten years his senior in experience of life in many of its phases.

Hesbia had little love for the country in general, and none for Blairavon in particular. She rather liked the idea of " papa having a place in Scotland," because the Queen had made the possession of such a retreat fashionable, and it gave her something to talk about in Liverpool. She certainly liked the somewhat baronial aspect of the old manor-house, especially when it was full of visitors ; but she hated the people around, for the old county families looked coldly on "the parvenus" at races and elsewhere. The ladies, she thought, were barely polite—almost insolent—to her, though her appearance, style of dress, her carriage, grooms and horses, were all certainly in most respects second to none that the three Lothians could produce.

The county dames disliked Hesbia Vere not the less that their sons and husbands both liked and admired her ; for the girl was artful, and a student in the art of attracting attention to the most minute degree. She knew exactly when and how to look, to smile, and to blush ; how to leave a sentence unfinished, so as to give it double power or meaning ; to droop her fine eyelids and then look up with soft or tender and childlike enquiry or with a bold and flashing glance ; to play with her rippling hair or her gloves ; to let her tiny foot, in its marvellous kid boot, peep out precisely at the proper time ; and she knew well when to adopt the tones of playful reproach, of gentle pleading, and of most singular pathos.

Bright and beautiful—most beautiful—were those

soft brown eyes of Hesbia Vere; but, strange to say, their smiles were neither pure nor holy. Cast together in the country with such a girl as this, after their first intimacy,—a girl with such a singular amount of individuality in her character and bearing, —poor Lennard Blair was certain to be helplessly lost.

Clasping her gloved hands upon his arm for a moment, she said.—

"Though glad to see you now, Mr. Blair, I must deplore the sad event which so suddenly brought you hither."

"And I have to thank you for many a kind visit to the poor old gentleman before it took place."

"I dare say you long expected it?"

"Yes—but when it did come——"

"Ah, of course—yes, yes—we know all that," interrupted Hesbia, whose mind had no turn for grave thoughts; "but I am glad you have come to lighten the days of my—own banishment, for such I consider life here."

"Even in the sweet season of summer?"

"Even in summer," she said, as they paused.

Two pretty hands cased in Houbigant's softest kids were playing with his Albert chain and the charms that dangled thereat. The position had its charm, and the moment was opportune, though he dared not attempt to make more of it; the very land he looked on, the giant elms overhead, no longer his own, but *hers*, somehow forebade it.

"Yes, I weary here," she resumed, as they again

walked onward; "but we have got a delightful box of books from Mudie's. Shall I send you over some?"

"Thanks; but I am sick of books, and while here would rather ramble on the green hill-slopes or in the leafy woods."

"How romantic! you are surely very much in love——"

"In love—oh, Hesbia!" he began impetuously.

"Yes—with Nature. My cousin Travice was to meet me here at the end of the Willow Loan, as you Scotch people queerly call it, but I see nothing of him."

Lennard's countenance fell, and without perceiving this,—for she was scanning all the neighbouring fields and the sunny landscape,—Hesbia resumed:

"What do you think Travice said about my foot, Mr. Blair?"

"That it is very handsome, of course."

"Yes; and that if I will lend him a shoe, he will fill it with champagne and drain it before all the gentlemen at the first hunting dinner."

"A fool!"

"Fie! he is only my cousin; and what cousins say or do can matter little." And as she spoke she smiled from under one of the daintiest parasols that ever shaded two bright coquettish eyes from the glare of a brilliant sun. "You must learn to master your piques, or they may master you."

"In many ways I am not my own master, and in

more I am a slave!" said Lennard, with a sudden gush of bitterness; "and so there are times when I find the duty of obedience somewhat of a task, and rail at fortune."

"We are all subordinate or inferior to some one in this world, Mr. Blair," replied Hesbia rather sententiously.

"True."

"But you talk oddly of duty, of obedience, of fortune: are you not a partner in papa's firm?"

"Yes; but to so small an amount that I am scarcely recognised as such, especially on 'Change; and am nevertheless obliged to be your papa's most obedient servant for the sum of two hundred pounds or so per annum. Of course he pays his butler an equal sum."

"Lennard Blair, do you not know that you are becoming very unpleasant?"

"Hesbia!"

"And positively quarrelling with me," she exclaimed, and her half-closed eyes glittered with pleasure rather than perplexity, for she saw that he was inspired by a jealousy of her cousin Cheatwood.

"I am not quarrelling with you, Miss Vere; nothing surely could be further from my mind, though there was a momentary bitterness in it."

"Why?"

"I was strangely brought up, Miss Vere;" said Lennard colouring, "and I was taught to think very differently from your city-bred boys, who are generally thoroughly practical, and not apt to cherish illusions."

"I understand—oh, yes! I know that your papa, poor man! always despised mine, because he had made his money in trade."

"Despise?"

"Yes."

"Ah, do not use a term so harsh."

"It was exceedingly behind the age, such a sentiment; but I know, too, that he actually hated him, simply because papa had acquired by purchase the lands and estate which he had not the prudence to preserve for himself, and, more than all, for you."

"Ah, had he but done so," Lennard was beginning with a glance of tender meaning, when she again interrupted him by saying, rapidly,—

"All this was not just; but the truth is, Mr. Blair, that our country gentlemen and great landholders, if not politicians, farmers, breeders of fat pigs and great poultry, or something of the kind, fall into foolish or vicious habits, and lose that on which so many set a store—their landed estates; their 'dirty acres,' as they are so fond of terming them."

The dark expression which had been gathering on Lennard's face deepened, when Hesbia sharply withdrew her arm from his, on the sudden approach of a gentleman who came slowly sauntering along the footpath, and whom she introduced to Lennard as her cousin, Mr. Travice Cheatwood.

They bowed, lifted their hats, and rather coldly surveyed each other; for Mr. Cheatwood proved to be his companion of the night express—the cool, impudent, and intrusive passenger from Liverpool; and now there was the old supercilious smile on his lips, but none in his eyes, as he coaxed his fair moustache and long goatee-beard, and said,—

"How d'ye do, Mr. Blair? Glad to see you, to make your acquaintance. Happy 'm sure."

"We have met before."

"Ah, yes—of course. In the Liverpool train I think it was."

"We begun rather unpleasantly."

"Let bygones be bygones. I think you a thoroughly good fellow," said Cheatwood, presenting his hand which Lennard shook; and, as he did so, he could see that though there was frankness in the words there was none in the manner of the speaker, in whose cold grey eyes he read an expression of concealed dislike, if not hostility, which led him to feel that an enemy was before him; for, through Hesbia's art, she had contrived to excite her cousin's jealousy of their friendship.

"And now that I have met Mr. Cheatwood, I shall not trespass further on your time, or lure you further from home, Mr. Blair," said Hesbia; "but how, are you alone, Travice? I thought the baronet was with you."

"Luckily I contrived to give him and that little lawyer fellow, Dabchick, the slip in the coppice, and come here without them."

"And why were you so long coming?"

" You wearied for me ?" said he gaily.

" You flatter yourself—absurd ! No such thing ! But why I say ?"

" Because an old muff in a livery coat, whom I met herding a cob, scarcely understood me when I inquired the way to Mr. Blair's diggings, which people hereabout call Aikwudlee it seems. Out of London, I find it is all Scotch, or some such dialect that no fellow can understand."

" Travice ! " exclaimed Hesbia, reddening, for she felt that her cousin's tone was brusque and offensive, and knew that the "muff" referred to, was poor old Steinie, who had been attentively grazing his dead master's pony. " Then Mr. Blair," she added, presenting her hand, " you will dine with us on the day after to-morrow. It is no party, remember ; of course, how could it be, on a two days' invitation— only ourselves and Lady Foster, whom you will find charming, though a sad woman, who never flirts, like me."

" I shall be most happy; I need not write ? "

" Not unless you wish to have the pleasure of in- diting the tiniest and pinkest of notes to me—ta, ta—good bye."

And kissing her hand with a bright glance, swiftly shot—but concealed from the watchful Travice, by the skilful mode in which she managed her parasol —a glance full of hidden meaning to Lennard, she took her cousin's arm, patting it with a gentle pressure, and swept away.

The parting glance, with all its brightness and

meaning fondness, failed, however, to reassure
Lennard Blair.

Why, thought he, did she with such nervous
haste withdraw her arm from his arm, on this cousin's
approach?

"The birds of the air, the beasts of the field,
the fishes of the sea have their instincts, and man
has his." So by a mysterious intuition—some instinct swift as thought or light—Lennard felt that
while he hated this man, he was in turn hated, and
that Travice Cheatwood was doomed to be his bane,
his enemy. He could not account for this intuitive
and mutual antipathy, but he read the certainty in
the cold keen eye of Cheatwood, and heard it in the
tone of his voice. It was the old aphorism of Dr.
Fell realized, and he felt like Romeo,—

> "My mind misgives,
> Some consequence, yet hanging in the stars,
> Shall bitterly begin his fearful date
> With this night's revels."

So this was the Travice Cheatwood of whom he
had so often heard among the clerks in Canning
Place as a blackleg, gambler, and tabooed jockey,
whose life since boyhood had been a career of
shrewd betting, sharp gambling, horse-racing, cock-
fighting, frequenting casinos, billiard rooms, hells,
and haunts of "the Fancy," with every species of
low dissipation. He was the only nephew of Mr.
Vere, and son of the late Mr. Cheatwood, whose
share in the business had long since been bought

up, though the name was retained in the firm, as it had been an old-established one in Liverpool, and was thought to sound well; for more than thirty years no name was better known on 'Change than "old Cheat," as he was named by his cotemporaries.

A reckless fortune-hunting cousin, passably good-looking, profoundly confident too, with a consummate knowledge of the world—Lennard's jealousy was roused to fever heat!

He knew that he had left Hesbia in dangerous hands, and the knowledge of her notorious propensity for flirtation, with the freedom of intercourse, the facilities afforded by their relationship and mutual residence in a large old rambling house like Blairavon, made him feel that he was on the eve of losing her for ever, if indeed he had not lost her already.

CHAPTER IX.

DOCTOR FEVERLEY.

AN implied but undeclared lover—an understood but unaccepted one, unaccepted in any other sense than as a species of privileged angler, Lennard Blair felt all the doubts and miseries of his position most keenly now, and resolved that he would, if possible, end them on the eveniug of the dinner at Blairavon ; and that if all hope failed him, then he should start at once for Liverpool. Indeed, he did not see very well how he could remain away much longer from his desk in Canning Place, and there was little doubt of Mr. Vere taking the first opportunity of giving a pretty pointed hint to that effect.

On the day subsequent to the interview just narrated, Elsie Graham summoned him to the dining-room windows, to see a cavalcade which swept on horseback along the road by Craigellon. There were Hesbia Vere, and another lady, attended by several gentlemen, among whom the old servant indicated the baronet, who seemed to be a tall, thin, ungainly man, Travice Cheatwood, and one or two others, adding,—

"Your father, poor man, Mr. Lennard, used to say that in her saddle Miss Vere had the worst seat of any lady in the county; and all the county kent how good a judge *he* was of such things. Set her up, indeed, wi' her laces and braws! But truly, as the Scriptures say, 'pride goeth before destruction.'"

All day Lennard had been conning, sorting or burning old letters and family papers, the cares and correspondence of the dead—mouldy and dusty relics of affections that have passed away — old mementos of a thousand kindly descriptions were there, among flue and cobwebs, in the drawers of his father's escritoire; antique trinkets and locks of hair—mute symbols of hearts that once were faithful, passionate, and true; a broken fan, a glove rolled in tissue-paper, a silver pomander ball, with its secret and forgotten story.

Pell-mell among farriery, and veterinary bills, and racing memoranda of Richard Blair's plumy days, cuttings from *Bell's Life* of hunting meets and so forth, were many letters of his uncle Lennard, written home when a boy at school or a student at college, and there were letters, too, which to the present Lennard seemed faded and old, yellow and strange, for they were those of his parents in the days of their courtship.

Would children yet unborn, in the days of after years, be looking with the same melancholy interest over the letters of himself and——well, yes, Hesbia Vere?

So he closed the escritoire, and began to ponder over his position again.

Often, as on the preceding day, had he trembled on the verge of a declaration, which was perhaps expected; but he shrunk from the attempt with an emotion of pride that mingled with a nervous timidity of ridicule or rejection. And *now*, for all that he knew to the contrary, some one of those guests who were at Blairavon—the dapper little lawyer, who bore the absurd name of Dabchick; the baronet, who was half suspected of being an adventurer; or Travice Cheatwood, who was both adventurer and knave,—might be crossing the rubicon and making the wealthy flirt his own. So, "tide what may," Lennard resolved that the evening of the dinner should, if possible, end all his troubles, and place their intimacy on a more defined basis, or destroy it altogether.

Anything was better than his painful uncertainty.

Seated at a window of the dining-room overlooking the little garden where old Steinie, who usually filled up his leisure time there, was raking and trimming, Lennard Blair had just come to this satisfactory state of determination, when a hand was laid on

his shoulder, and the cheerful voice of Dr. Feverley
said—

"Still mooning, Blair. Come, rouse yourself, my
friend; I have some news for you."

"News—of what?"

"I am to dine at Blairavon, and you too, my
note mentions. Miss Vere adds that in a postscript,
where ladies have the reputation of referring to
that which is uppermost in their thoughts," Dr.
Feverley continued.

"Your presence will certainly add to my pleasure."

"Who else are going; do you know?" asked
Feverley, who had always an eye to practice.

"None but their visitors, Miss Vere said."

"Ah! you have seen her, then?"

"She brought me her own note."

"Ah!" and Feverley paused with a quizzical
expression of eye. "I feel dull this evening;
have been worried all day with two bad cases at the
colliery village; a miner's head terribly contused by
a fall in the great pit, and another of fracture
through the condyles of the humerus, so I have
just dropped in to smoke a pipe with you, thinking
you might be lonely."

Now, Steinie Hislop who, on seeing the Doctor
arrive had hastened from the garden and assumed
his shabby old livery coat, to act a new part, appeared in the room, and, unordered, brought the

decanters of port and sherry to the table, just as
had been his wont in the old Laird's time, when
Cheyne of the Haughs or any other visitor dropped
in ; and Feverley being, as he said, low spirited,
did not require much pressure to help himself to a
glass of the fine old madeira, which had been for
years in its cobwebby bin—one of the chief treasures
of Richard Blair's diminished household and curtailed
luxuries.

Though the "Vere set" were not the most distinguished in the county, the invitation to dine at
Blairavon had been to poor Doctor Feverley a
source of much real pleasure and satisfaction. Mr.
Vere had been one of the two or three grand
parochial patrons who occasionally employed him to
physic their servants, or even a child or so in some
very mild case indeed ; for in every serious one,
though Feverley was a very clever fellow, metro-
politan skill was alone relied on ; but here had
come a special invitation to a friendly and family
dinner.

It made the poor and modest young fellow as
happy almost as a young girl going to her first ball ;
and even now his affectionate old mother—her face
radiant with pleasure—was busy in preparing, with
her own tremulous hands, one of three dress shirts
of which her son's thrifty wardrobe could boast.

Perceiving that, in his flow of spirits, the Doctor
was disposed to rally him about Hesbia Vere,

Lennard prepared at once to turn the tables on him.

"There is a Lady Foster—a very pretty woman, she would seem—residing at Blairavon," said the Doctor.

"And rich, no doubt. Won't you try your luck, Feverley?"

"What, I—a poor dispensary doctor?"

"Why not? you are just the very man. Let us see; the 'inconsolable affliction of a widow of twenty, besieged by a lover of thirty,' that is about your mark, Feverley."

"How you run on, Blair; you forget that, unfortunately, there is a barrier."

"A canonical one?"

"Rather," said the Doctor, curtly. "The lady has a husband."

"By Jove! I thought she was a widow from the way Hesbia——"

"Who?"

"Miss Vere, I mean, spoke of her as being a sad little woman, who never flirted, and so forth."

"I have not met with either her or her husband. They have just arrived at Blairavon on a visit, and appear to be total strangers in this part of Scotland."

"Well, apart from her, I think a wife would be a great advantage to a parochial medical man. It is a recommendation for an extended practice, to be married, isn't it, Feverley?"

Feverley sighed and shook his head, while a gloomy expression came over his usually open and cheerful face.

"My exchequer is not a flourishing one, and the mineral well is a severe opposition to its increase. I have my mother—dear old soul!—to attend to my wants, while I attend to hers, and I am as happy as—as——"

"A king," suggested Lennard.

"Happier than some kings, perhaps, for I am now perfectly content."

"But marriage——"

"Don't talk of it, I pray you! I was once nearly trying my luck that way, but I shall never, never do so again."

"The bottle stands with you."

"Thanks," said Feverley, helping himself.

"Did the lady jilt you?"

"No."

"Poor Feverley—she died then?"

"No."

"She married another?"

"No."

"What on earth happened?" asked Lennard, with growing surprise.

"Another married her."

"What difference does that make?"

"Not much to the ear, perhaps; but there is a great difference in the sense," replied Feverley, as he drained his glass of wine, to fill and inadvertently empty it again, as if to drown some unpleasant thought. "In many ways I have endured much in my time, Blair; yet I am not many years older than yourself, being barely thirty; but there have been hours when, in the bitterness of my heart, the lines of Milton occurred, and his words rose to my lips,—

"Did I request the maker from the clay
    To form me man?"

and when I have asked of myself, why I was born into the world, and for what purpose?"

"And was a love-affair the cause of this?"

"A love-affair, but one full of profound sorrow, suffering, and wrong — yea, and sin too," said Feverley, in a broken voice, while covering his face with his hands, though the twilight had deepened so much that the wainscoted dining-room was almost dark, and the grove of Scottish firs without stood like giant trees of bronze against the ruby and amber-coloured sky of the west.

"It seems hard for you here, to have a life of loneliness before you," said Lennard, after a pause.

"Not Venus herself could tempt me into matrimony now," replied Feverley, with energy; "it would seem but a second marriage in which I could offer only the mockery of love—all freshness of feeling having passed out of me."

There was a considerable pathos in the voice of the young Doctor; and Lennard, circumstanced as he was with Hesbia Vere, felt a kindred chord vibrate keenly in his breast.

" Feverley," said he, " I beg your pardon, if, by a heedless jest or thoughtless question, I have brought a forgotten sorrow back to memory."

" Forgotten—oh, it can never be forgotten ! But how could you know what you had probed ? "—he breathed quickly as he spoke—" how could you see the shadow that has been thrown upon my life, or the dear memory that is enthroned in my inner heart, and shall never pass from thence but with my life ? " continued Feverley.

Lennard was sincerely grieved for the emotion he had excited; and therefore, to draw the Doctor from his sad thoughts, he spoke of the dark story of his uncle Lennard; of his being found in the lochlet at Craigellon, on the alleged unlucky day of the family; of his own great secret—his love for Hesbia Vere, his fears, and doubts of its success, and so forth.

" But she whom I loved and who loved me so well—too well, perhaps—was a very different girl from Hesbia Vere," said Feverley, bluntly.

" Different ? " said Lennard, not quite liking some-.thing in the Doctor's tone.

"Ah, yes; Mildred Montgomerie was altogether another style of girl."

"In appearance?"

"In face and stature, in manner and bearing. Miss Vere has the reputation of being a beautiful coquette—whether justly so, I know not; she is a brilliant and sparkling girl, with admirers ever by her side; but she that I—I loved was a soft and tender, a fragile and gentle girl, as unlike Hesbia Vere as a modest little violet differs from a full-blown moss-rose."

There was something still more unpleasing in this speech to Lennard, but he knew not what to say; and now, after a pause, Feverley, who, under the influence of the wine, good fellowship, and a real liking for Lennard Blair, had been seized by one of those fits of communicativeness which possess all frank fellows at times, said,—

"I'll tell you my story, Blair, and how it came to pass that I am but a poor country practitioner, content to vegetate here at Blairavon; and when you have heard it, I shall be surprised if you do not think my love-affair was a very sad one."

So what the young Doctor related deserves, at least, an entire chapter to itself.

CHAPTER X.

THE COUSIN LOVERS.

MY father was, like myself, a medical man, and though, like myself, he wrote the honourable letters M.D., F.R.C.P.E. after his name, he had a difficulty in procuring a lucrative practice; and, having married early a Miss Montgomerie, the pretty sister of a brother student, he was fain to accept an appointment in Jamaica, and there I was born, in the land of sugar, coffee, cotton, and the yellow fever.

I was one of five children, but the sole survivor; as the rest of the little brood perished in succession, of ailments peculiar to the island; so I was sent home to be reared and educated by my maternal uncle, whose residence, Monkwood Moat, is an old baronial place of the Scottish and English fighting times, situated in a beautiful part of the Merse.

Though young Montgomery of the Moat never forgave his sister for marrying the poor medical practitioner who had been his friend at their old

Alma Mater, and with whom he had chummed for
years, and "ground" together for many a weary
night, he could scarcely decline to receive her son,
the poor little boy whom she had named Frank in
honour of him, and who had come so far to avoid
the pests of which his brothers and sisters perished.

My uncle, Frank Montgomerie, was not a wealthy
man; he had not taken high degrees at college, and
he too had made a poor marriage; but then his
wife was a daughter of one of the best families on
the Scottish Border, for he was a man who, like
the late Mr. Blair, set prodigious store upon crests
and mottoes, on name, heraldic honours, and so
forth; and, being vain of his descent from the Montgomeries of Skelmorlie and Eglinton, had learned
to look with lofty contempt upon his sister's husband,
the poor doctor who was broiling among planters,
niggers, and maroons in Jamaica, and who could
only boast of the common pedigree of all, from that
respectable old kitchen gardener who handled his
spade in Eden.

If his marriage had been a high one, it had
neither proved lucrative nor happy. His wife was
much of an invalid, and died in giving birth to their
only child, a daughter named after her, Mildred
Home Montgomerie, and since that event my uncle
had secluded himself in the old house at Monkwood,
where he rarely saw visitors, and more rarely went
abroad.

So there were we, the cousins, a boy and girl—I a year or so older than Milly—the only source of noise, merriment, or smiles in the lonely old house which was to be, for an indefinite period, my home. We soon learned to love each other as brother and sister, or something of that kind; not that any one taught us to do so, for we required no artificial tutelage; it came to us naturally, this child-like love—this sentiment of mutual regard and endearment.

Though somewhat cold in his manner, Uncle Frank was always kind to me, and would often smile kindly when he saw me playing about in the same rooms and places where his sister—now far, far away—had lived her happy girl life.

Happy, happy were those years of my boyhood at the old house of Monkwood, in the companionship of that sweet cousin Milly!

The mansion-house is situated amid the most beautiful portion of the Merse, some miles inland from its coast of rocky precipices, and under the shadow of Clinthill, the highest peak of the lovely Lammermuir range.

I shall never see it more, for never again could I look on the old Moat of Monkwood; yet in all its features and details the beloved place comes vividly before me, with its half-castellated outline, and a turret or two roofed with grey stone, peeping up above the chestnut groves.

Around it are silent tarns or lochlets—remnants they may be of the vast marsh from which the county took its ancient name—with masses of water-lilies floating on the surface, and islets of bulrushes where the coot and heron linger. Dark clumps of old forest, too, are there, such as that round the Hair-stane Rig, varying the great expanse of green pasture land, or the upland slopes, where, when the lapwing comes, the harbinger of spring, the young grain first begins to sprout, and where it first ripens into golden yellow, in the early harvest time.

In the heats of summer we found plenty of shady places wherein to lurk amid the old forest trees, or the groves of drooping willows, by the little lakes where we were never weary of wandering in quest of childish adventures, or of nuts, berries, and butterflies; or setting lilies and harebells afloat upon the mountain-burn that came brawling from whence and to where we knew not, though it was only flowing from the green slopes of the Lammer-muirs towards the German sea.

Happy times were those; we had the same tutor, the same tasks, the same occupations, and the same amusements. Milly never grew weary of them; neither did I; nor did we ever weary of each other.

Milly was a rosy, laughing girl then—the picture of a joyous, blooming Hebe; her dark eyes sparkling with health and happiness, and her dark hair falling in a cascade about her ivory neck and shoulders.

A little time—you may foresee the period that was coming—and we would sit silent for hours, while I played with that dark silky hair, and heaved strange sighs in my heart, and felt deep unuttered thoughts of—I scarcely knew what. But childhood was passing away, an older phase of existence followed it, and we were beginning to wake from our dream that all the world was contained in Monkwood Moat, and that the hemisphere was bounded by the Lammermuirs and Firth of Forth; and so were launching into a newer, a more delicious, but dangerous dream of life, that made each, and each only, all the world to the other.

I was sixteen when my West-Indian remittances began to fail; my uncle Montgomerie cared little for that; but one morning a letter arrived with a seal and edging of black.

My father, whose face and figure were little more than a vague and dreamy memory now, was dead!

Over-worked in his practice when the cholera had broken out, he had died at his post in a great public hospital, and my mother was left in such meagre circumstances that she resolved not to return home until she had realized some money or property my father had, or was to have had, and so forth—I never could make it out exactly; but for five years she remained in Jamaica battling with the law courts, in the hope of achieving this realization, and prior to her return many changes had taken place with me.

By the time this crash came, I had learned to love my cousin Mildred with all the strength and depth of an enthusiastic and imaginative boy's first passion, and certainly her beauty was calculated to inspire it. By the time she was eighteen, much of the girlish bloom of her hoydenish days had been toned down, or changed in character. Her face was small, pale, and colourless, very white and pure, for somewhat of her mother's delicacy had descended to her, and the transparent cheek would flush upon the least excitement. She had marvellously delicate and minute features, eyes of the softest and deepest violet, with lashes of wondrous length, that imparted to her face a charming expression of modesty and gentleness.

Her figure was, perhaps, somewhat too *petite*. She was timid among strangers, though we rarely saw any at Monkwood, and she seemed to cling with confidence only to me, for her father's manner was more repelling than prepossessing; yet he was intensely vain of her beauty, and of the delicate form of her hands, feet, and ears, which were, he would pompously say, "such models of perfection as could only come of the blood of the Montgomeries of Skelmorlie and Eglinton."

We had learned to know that we were no longer children, and had become lovers, when the time so

dreaded arrived that I had to choose a line in life—
a profession, an occupation.   Like other boys I had
my visions of soldiering, of sailoring, and of having,
like Robinson Crusoe, a snug little island of my
own, with Milly as a companion in lieu of Friday;
but those schoolday whims were past now, and so I
resolved to adopt an avocation which has ever led
the van in all works of charity and benevolence—
and nowhere more nobly than in our native Scotland—the practice of medicine, and to be, as my
poor father had been before me, a doctor.

So sweet Milly Montgomerie and I were to be
separated at last !

I remember the time when our airy bubble burst
—when the fairy palace in which we had been
dwelling passed away like that of Aladdin, and our
first real sorrow came upon us.

Summer had come.   Over the green braes and
upland slopes the old limes and chesnut-trees were
casting their deepest shadows; the white water-
lilies and the dusky coots were floating on the lovely
blue tarns ; the wild flowers and the gueldre-roses
bloomed beside the old deep-rutted roads, where,
in other times, many an English beeve and hirsel
had been goaded northward by the wild moss-
troopers.

The atmosphere was laden with all the rich odours
of the season, and all nature around Monkwood
Moat looked as it ever did in its summer beauty

and the sun shone as brightly, but the hearts of Milly and I were sad.

" You know, Milly darling," said I—for the theme of the sweet relationship, the more tender tie that was to be one day between us, had long since been exhausted—" that I have now learned to deplore the want of some useful profession, which would render me—I should say us, dearie—*us* independent."

" But what need have you of a profession, or for slaving at college to learn one?" she asked, impetuously.

" All men do something for their livelihood, Milly."

" All men who are poor."

" And am I rich?" I asked, sadly.

" You have me," she replied, laying her head upon my shoulder; and I covered her little face with kisses. " Listen to me, Frank," she resumed, after a pause; " we have Monkwood Moat—at least papa has—and is not that quite the same?"

" I fear he does not think so—and certainly never would if he knew all. In his heart, and in his strange antiquated ideas, he despises the name and blood I inherit from my poor father, and has repeatedly hinted that I should push my way in India, under the patronage of his friend Mr. Wharton, or in some of the distant colonies."

" No—no—no! this is not to be thought of for a moment. Here have we stayed for years, and here

shall we ever stay, dear Frank; yes, all the days of
our lives, as the story-books say, and watch papa as
he grows old. It will do him good to see us; oh,
so happy, as we shall always be!"

This scheme was not an impossible or unpleasing
one; but our fate was not in our own hands. Uncle
Montgomerie had detected enough to make him
resolve on our immediate separation; and long after
that dread time came to pass, it was my delight, when
alone, to turn the soul inward, and live over and
over again the last interview we had together, and
to treasure the words and the wishes of my generous
and guileless cousin Milly.

He had seen enough, I say, to bring about my
immediate departure for Edinburgh, as he had other
views concerning his daughter, whom he was actually
reserving as a wife for his friend Judge Wharton,
who was returning from India with wealth that was
reputed to be enormous; and though he made me a
tolerably handsome allowance for my maintenance
at college, he proved, in the end, the true melodramatic father with a "flinty heart." Sternly he
said to Milly,—

"Too long has Monkwood been a scene of fooling
for a moonstruck youth, with a spasmodic attack of
the tender passion for a silly girl who is barely past
that age when every damsel fancies herself in love
with her music-master, however stout, old, or
married the man may be; and I have sworn," he

added, " that though the nameless beggar, Feverley, stole my sister, the beggar's son shall not add to the injury by stealing my daughter!"

These were bitter words; and when they were communicated to me in a letter from my poor mother—who was still lingering in Jamaica after that imaginary property, for my behoof rather than her own—they sank deeply and sorrowfully into my heart.

However, I knew nothing of my uncle's mood of mind; and looking forward only to college vacation, when I should be free to rush back to Milly and the happiness of Monkwood Moat, I matriculated at Edinburgh in October, and became one of the most energetic of the many medical students at the *Academia Jacobi VI. Scotorum Regis;* on the grand, deep archways, the stately Doric columns, and the vast and silent quadrangle of which I was wont to gaze with something of profound respect—aye, and love too; for there on its balustraded terraces, and amid the hum of those lofty and crowded class-rooms, had my father, in all the hope and ardour of youth, studied and toiled before me; and now he was lying, the victim of his professional enthusiasm, far away in a West-Indian grave.

Self-conceit, the curse of your provincial Scotsman and Englishman too, was not, perhaps, my greatest peril; though I could not believe myself to be quite the paragon my mother thought me in childhood, and Cousin Milly, during the happy years at Monkwood Moat.

I remember that, on the very day I matriculated, I gave a jeweller in Princes Street a lock of Milly's dark hair to put in a pretty locket for me. Whether the trinket I selected was too small, or that I was rash in leaving the treasured tress with him, I know not now; but on receiving back the lock, it was severed, cut in *two*; and then a dim foreboding came over me that something of evil to our love would happen, and little more than boy though I was, I trembled in my heart. Was this a weakness, or an intuition of the future?

God only knows.

From that day forward, I plunged deep into study, into hard reading and attendance at the classes for the preliminary examinations in arts. It was some time before disgust in the dissecting-room was mastered by curiosity, enthusiasm, and a genuine wonder at the marvels of Nature. I had a chum who read with me, and we ground each other up in everything that has been published of late years, from "Fyfe's Anatomy" and "Bell, on the Bones," to the seventh edition of "Quain's Elements."

Milly and I corresponded in secret, through the medium of the village post-office; and we both looked forward impatiently to the vacation time, which came in due course; but brought with it a letter from my uncle, informing me that I was to

spend the period between it and returning to my
studies either in Edinburgh or at Monkwood as I
chose; but if at the latter, I should be alone, as he
and Milly were to pass that portion of the year in
the south of England.

This was a shock and a disappointment on which
I had not calculated. To linger on in Edinburgh
amid the dust of its hot and empty streets in summer was galling in the extreme; but still more
galling would it be to go back to lonely Monkwood
House, where—Ichabod, Ichabod, the glory had departed!—Milly was no longer there. So I remained
in our northern metropolis, a dreary residence for a
total stranger.

But the summer passed, and brown autumn came
with its studies and its work, and I made the most
rapid progress at the university.

My uncle now fairly gave me to understand, when
one day I met him in town, that for the future—at
least until I passed and graduated—I was *not* to
present myself at Monkwood. I understood completely what that meant, and from that moment
there was a species of secret warfare maintained
between us.

I know that I was in error and to blame for
acting as I had done, but the love of Milly blinded
me to every scruple, and on every occasion in which
I could spare time, I took the rail for Berwickshire,
and contrived to have many a tender and delicious

interview with her, unknown to all save ourselves, at our old haunts, by the tarns where the lilies floated and the wild ducks squatted among the bulrushes, by the burn that gurgled under its hawthorn bowers from the Lammermuirs towards the sea, by the Hair-stane Rig, where the men of the Merse held their battle trysts of old, and in the deep dark groves of Monkwood.

We had but one hope, that when I graduated, I should be more thoroughly my own master, and then we should be married; and each time that I left her, with her tears and kisses lingering on my cheek, I returned to the drudgery of study with fresher ardour, thinking only of the happiness that awaited me when the term of probation was complete; when I could write the magical letters "M.D." after my name, and my gentle, delicate, and ladylike Milly would take upon herself the vows of a wife, and, more than ever, be all the world to me.

These hopes and fears kept me safely amid all the dissipations and follies incident to a student's life at the great Scottish university; and erelong I had but one session to pass before my final examination.

I can well remember the terrors of the preliminary, though the most simple one; from "writing an account extending to not more than two pages," of my usual place of residence (in which I accurately described Monkwood, not omitting cousin Milly, (to the great amusement of the professors), on through Latin, French, and German, and so forth, till I came to chemistry and the institutes of medicine.

One morning two letters of evil import reached me; for misfortunes are said never to come alone. One was from Mildred, informing me that I had a rival in the field, in the person of her father's old friend Mr. Philip Wharton, who had been long a Sudder judge in India, a political resident at the court of his Highness the Nizam of Rumchunder Chowry, for turning whose affairs topsy-turvy till the intervention of the Company's troops became necessary, he had been made a K.S.I., and now came home with an enormous fortune.

The little cloud that was no bigger than a man's hand on our horizon, was fated to spread fast after this.

The second letter announced the return of my mother from the West Indies, broken in health and prospects, for the affair of the property (whatever it was) had turned out a total failure, and that for the future all her dependence must be on *me*.

Still I did not let my courage sink, but worked away with renewed ardour, for Milly's subsequent letters were always reassuring. Wharton, a man old enough to be her father, and yellow as a marigold, had proposed for her hand in the first week of his arrival, and, of course, had been refused; but it

was evident that he and her father were in league
and consultation about the matter. He had a leave
of two years from India, and could give her plenty
of time. Her letters, I have said, were reassuring;
yet, if too long a period passed without my receiving
one, I became inspired by a natural uneasiness—a
rather unreasonable jealousy.

Might it not be, I asked of myself, that the attentions of a stranger, even of a man well on in years,
and the novelty thereof, with the flattering prospect
of all that his wealth could afford her—the pictures
he could draw of Indian luxury and Oriental
splendour—might lure her to forget the boy-lover
of her guileless youth, and of the pleasant days in
Monkwood Moat?

In these surmises I did my beloved Mildred a
cruel wrong.

And yet, with such thoughts as these to torture
me at times, I had to go deep into surgery, general
pathology, materia medica, and be able to explain to
a nicety the differences between the cell theories of
Schwann, Goodsir, and Huxley.

My small allowance had been reduced by remittances sent to my mother in Jamaica, I had contracted several petty debts in the city, and medical
works, it must be remembered, are somewhat dearer
than lighter literature, but I had been promised a
handsome sum from Milly's father on the day I
graduated; and with that promise were some un-

mistakable hints about the scarcity of medical men
in certain colonies—anything to be handsomely rid
of me, and that if I went abroad he would settle an
allowance on the now penniless widow, my mother.

At last came the day of the final examination,
with its consequent doubts, terrors, tremors, parched
tongues, fears, and hopes, before which even those
of the lover dwindle away.

I went, of course, accurately attired in black, the
sombre livery of physic, law, divinity, and too often
the cloak of hyprocrisy and prosperous corruption in
the modern Athens. My grinder had done wonders
for me; he had put words in my mouth and new
ideas into my head. I wrote my own thesis, however, which is more than some fellows do.

I was, somehow, very confident; I had worked
hard, and my famous essay on the " Removal of a
cauliflower excrescence from the brain of a Bailie of
Edinburgh, by means of the galvano-caustic wire,"
and on the "Amputation of the *os-coccygis* of a
Manx cat, without the use of chloroform," did the
affair for me, and took the examiners by storm.

One ill-natured and surly professor of surgery
was weak enough to dance upon my little production,
and tear it to pieces before his class, as an impertinent intrusion on his own line of business; but as
he had already done the same to one of the greatest
works on surgery, I consoled myself, though he
pressed especially hard upon me.

Well, I passed with flying colours, and was Francis Feverley, M.D.; and that day, amid the congratulations of many poor fellows who had been "plucked," I came forth into the quadrangle. I seemed to tread on air, and felt myself several inches taller as I issued from the great archway of the college into the sunlighted and bustling thoroughfare without.

Subsequent events came so thick and fast upon me that the glories of the capping day, the 1st of August, in the old Academia Jacobi VI., when I figured in a black cloth hood, lined with crimson silk; and those of the graduating dinner, with its dissipation and fun, passed away like a dream. A jovial dinner it is too, even to be attended by those who matriculate only to throw dust in the eyes of the old folks at home, who cut the anatomical class as offensive, beyond the reach of Rimmel or aromatic vinegar, and hate the lectures as a stupid bore.

Amid the buzz and gabble round me—of Titjiens or Mario's song; of chloroform and acupressure; of splendid cases and excision of tongues, tumours and excrescences; the girls at the last assembly; of the University Eleven; the crack shot of the rifle company, the speeches, toasts, and so forth, I thought only of Monkwood and of her whose good wishes were so dearer by far than even those of the hearty fellows to whom I was about to bid farewell—for we, who for years had studied side by side in the same class-rooms, were about to separate and be scattered in every land under the sun.

My health was proposed by a brother sawbones, with the earnest wish that I might "settle in a fine unhealthy locality; that after opium and calomel failed, I should always trust to nature for the rest." Handsome things were said about the cauliflower excrescence, and then the toast was drunk with all the honours amid a noisy chorus.

"Fill ye up a brimming glass, jolly brother students;
  Toss the bumper ere it pass, jolly brother students!"

On returning to my lodgings, fagged, weary, and excited, a letter from Monkwood awaited me—but not one of gratulation on my success, information of which I had duly telegraphed. My uncle simply stated that my correspondence with Milly had been discovered; that, in consequence of my duplicity, disobedience, and ingratitude, I should not, from that hour, receive another shilling from him; that any debts I had contracted I might pay how and best I chose; and that, on peril of something vague and terrible, I was never more to address my cousin, who was about to return again to the south of England.

This was a crusher, on the very day of my crowning success, too!

Some time elapsed before I took in the whole situation. I found myself encumbered by debts,

which, though not great, were great enough for me;
Milly on the eve of being carried off; my mother
on her way home; my only stay gone; and I had
but a few shillings in the world.

I was bewildered and benumbed by the shock, but
had all the next day for reflection. It was, I remember, Sunday, which in Scotland seems as the
burial-day of the past week, rather than the first of
a new one. To raise money for my exigences, I
could see but one way—to take the humble situation
(which a friend offered me) of surgeon of a whaler,
which was to sail from Leith for the North seas in
about a month; so September came, and found me
still idling in Edinburgh, till a note from Milly,
written too evidently under extreme agitation,
reached me. It contained but a few lines, and had
been dispatched in secret at a distant country post-
office :—

" DEAREST, DEAREST FRANK,—

" Something terrible is about to happen to me
—my father is driving me mad—yes, literally mad !
Come to me instantly. Each evening after dusk, or
at midnight, when all are in bed, I shall be in the
arbour at the end of the garden. For Heaven's
sake, dear, dear Frank, do not delay coming to meet
your own brokenhearted,

" MILLY MONTGOMERIE."

The sunset of the next evening saw me looking down on Monkwood Moat and coppice, from the green slope of the Lammermuirs.

It was the season when the first leaves begin to fall, and "there was a Sabbath stillness in the autumn air"—all so still, indeed, that nothing seemed moving but the grey smoke that curled up from the chimneys of the house amid the brown foliage. There was no sound in the solitude, and I could almost hear the beating of my own heart.

It was one of those lovely evenings, when, as Longfellow has it—

> " There seems a beautiful spirit breathing now
> Its mellow richness on the clustered trees,
> And, from a beaker full of richest dyes,
> Pouring new glory on the autumn woods,
> And dipping in warm light the pillared clouds."

The memory of all the joys and hopes and happiness of the past—of our many stolen interviews, all the sweeter for being so—came welling up strongly and vividly within me, as I looked on each familiar feature of that lovely landscape, which was now before me, as I fully believed, for the last time.

The autumn evening appeared of interminable length, and the dusk as if it would never come. Slowly the shadows deepened in the russet woods, and the last rays faded from the wavy range of hills; then, leaping a wall, with which I was familiar, I made my way towards the shady old arbour in the garden.

Milly was not there, so I sat down to await her in the place where we had so often played together in childhood and met as lovers in later years. Every leaf that rustled caused me to start in expectation of her approach; but the dewy evening deepened into night without her appearing at our trysting-place. Was she ill? Had our intention been suspected? Had she been carried off? What was this terrible event that was about to happen, and of which she dared not, apparently, trust herself to write?

In torturing suspense, I watched the lights in the windows of the old house go out, as they were extinguished in succession, when the inmates retired to rest; and, ere the quaint façade of Monkwood was sunk in an obscurity and darkness that made its masses blend with the surrounding trees, I heard midnight struck by the clock of the distant village church.

With a plaid or shawl thrown loosely over her head and shoulders, Milly came softly and swiftly to join me, and threw herself hysterically on my neck and breast. The pallor on her face, as I viewed it by the starlight, terrified me; her sobs were deep and painful, while her eyes were inflamed and sparkling with combined anger and sorrow.

In a few words she told me all; that Mr. Wharton had again proposed for her hand and been accepted by her father, who was now having the marriage settlements drawn up; that she had urged in vain the disparity of years; in vain that she did not love Mr. Wharton, and never could do so, even as a friend; but resentment at me and Wharton's great wealth were incentives which rendered her father, a man at all times proud and passionate, now systematically inexorable!

She had stooped to appeal to Mr. Wharton, and in her desperation to save herself from him, had avowed her love for me, and our engagement; but this appeal was made in vain; he had only laughed and said she "would get over her girlish love in time, and when once she was in India, would forget all about it."

She would fly from the house, she told me amid her heavy sobs, but where was she to go with credit to herself? She was without money, or means, or friends who would receive her, and thus her whole dependence was on *me!*

Domestic persecution does not exist in the pages of romance alone. Here, by a studied system, it had done its worst upon poor Mildred Montgomerie; and when I told her how I was situated—that I had certainly passed as M.D., but without avail as yet; that I was now more desperate and penniless than ever, and on the eve of sailing for the Greenland seas,—her agony seemed to reach a climax.

" Oh ! Frank, Frank, my sole hope, my last dependence was on you, and yet you will not take me
away—you will not save me from him or from myself, and make me your wife—your wife, dearest
Frank, as I have so often promised to be,—yes,
Frank, in this very bower ! "

Her words wrung my heart.

" Silent still ? " she resumed. " Oh ! Frank, hear
me. We have loved each other so long and so
dearly—and so dearly do we love each other still,
that we cannot be separated. The tie between us is
too strong and yet so tender. Think of me being
sold to that old man—to lie in his arms and not in
yours ! Do not desert me ; say that you will not—
another fortnight and it will be too late—too late—
all will then be over, and I—far, far away from
you ! "

Much more did she say as we sat in the bower
entwined in a close embrace. It was too dark for
me to see the pale, passionate little face; but I felt
how wildly her heart was beating against my own.
There was a storm of resentment against her father
and the rich intruder, conflicting with the hot
young love and pitying tenderness that inspired me;
but I felt myself powerless, because I was penniless,
and anger made me feel revengeful.

The first gleam of day was brightening on the
summits of the Lammermuirs when we separated ;
she stole back to the house, and I darted into the

woods. We had promised to meet in the bower next night; but a thousand times better had it been if we had never met more!

I loitered in the neighbourhood of Monkwood, and night after night we met in that old and secluded bower, where she would lie for hours in my arms, till, out of the dense obscurity of the place, I could see her little white features, her delicate profile and the pearly teeth through the parted lips that smiled no more—even on me—though the eyes and hearts and souls of both of us were still inspired by the most passionate love, a love sharpened by the blind desperation of our circumstances.

Daily in the great world around us we see hopes blighted and affections crushed by poverty; marriages contracted for money or broken off by the lack of it, and some that are about to be made for gold replaced by those that are made for love; but one might well suppose that, in an age so advanced, coercion in such matters had ceased; yet it was not so in our case.

I cannot tell you all that followed—even my voice fails me, as you may hear; there was no eye on our midnight meetings save One, and that was forgotten.

*　　*　　*　　*　　*　　*

It seemed to me that at our last adieu Milly was more composed; but an illness came upon her—a fever occasioned by grief, agitation, and the chill hours of meeting; I heard that her marriage was delayed, and, in the hope that it might yet be so for a longer period, I sailed as surgeon of the Leith whaler for the North sea.

I was several months absent—a longer period than I could have anticipated; but when far away in the Greenland seas, when the sharp peaks of Spitzbergen were rising against the stars, or in Davis's Straits, where blocks of ice and masses of rock lie mingling on the desert shore, my heart was ever at home by bonnie Monkwood Moat; and in my dreams at night, those meetings in the dark arbour, the sweet, pale profile, the passionate kisses and endearments came back to me with a strange distinctness that gave alike exquisite pleasure and pain.

Our ship was the first of the Scottish fleet of whalers that, after a successful fishing, hauled up for home. The Northern Isles were soon passed; a few days after we sighted the Red Head of Angus; and ere many hours were over, I saw the white waves climbing the stern bluff of St. Abb, and the evening sunlight shedding a ruddy glory on the long wavy line of the blue Lammermuirs.

I was up aloft in the fore-cross-trees, for my eyes were full of tears, and I was ashamed lest any of the crew should detect my emotion.

The next night saw me at Monkwood, but, alas! it was already occupied by strangers.

"The proprietor had let it and gone to London; and Miss Montgomery, that *was*, had sailed with her husband, Judge Wharton, for India."

Such was the brief information a servant gave me, and so ended my romance of love; for, from that time—save once through a newspaper—I have heard no more of Milly Montgomerie.

"She died?" asked Lennard, starting as the Doctor paused abruptly in his story (which he had no doubt begun under a momentary impulse), for his voice became strangely broken by emotion.

"Died—no, God forbid!"

"And this newspaper notice —— "

"Was the birth of a son prematurely at Bombay; and then did I feel that, if possible, she was indeed Wharton's wife and more than ever lost to me!"

CHAPTER XI.

BLAIRAVON HOUSE.

ON the day of the dinner-party, for the first time
after the lapse of several years, did Lennard
Blair find himself turning his footsteps up the stately
avenue that leads to the house of Blairavon, through
an archway on which was carved, in the days when
James V. was wont to hunt the stag in Falkland
woods, the escutcheon of the Blairs, to wit: on a
saltier nine mascles of the field, and in chief a mullet
of eight points; over all a stag's head *caboshed;* but
a luxuriant coat of ivy hid all the sculpture now, so
Mr. Vere was pleased to permit it to remain, or perhaps
had forgotten its existence.   Even the supporters,
two of those wild men or demi-savages which are
peculiar to the ancient heraldry of Scotland, were
completely hidden.

Close up to the low platform of rock on which
Blairavon stands are some trees which are the remnant of a forest of the Coille-dhonean, or Men of
the Wood—a forest old, perhaps, as the days of the

Roman Wall. The oaks are aged and hollow now; but against their gnarled stems the boars have ground their tusks and the snow-white bulls their horns in the times of old; and under them, in autumn time, the dark brown leaves lie more than ankle deep.

One of those quaint old places of the years bordering on the Reformation—mansions which are scattered over Scotland and the Isles by thousands—Blairavon was an instance of the first improvement which took place in domestic architecture when the gloomy old castle or lonely peel-tower on the mountain slope, gave place to the gable-ended chateau built in the sheltered glen, but also calculated for security, so far as it could be imparted by strong walls, narrow windows, and iron bars;—hence the striking Scoto-French style of architecture which is peculiar to the country.

Blairavon, with its high, crowstepped gables, and three turrets with steep slated roofs like those of an old chateau by the Loire or Garonne, has a bold and pleasing outline among the venerable timber, the grey rocks and green hills which surround it; and the mind is carried back to the dark days of turmoil, of English invasion, and domestic feud, when its inmates

"Carved at the meal with gloves of steel,
And drank the red wine through the helmet barred."

I.   K

In conformity with some ancient superstition, the masons who built it are said to have mixed in their mortar the blood of those animals which were killed for their food and of the wild beasts of the adjacent forest, that the work might be more lasting. It stood bravely enough in its massive strength; but no more for the Blairs.

Iron gratings and massive window-frames had given place to sheets of plate-glass; and many alterations—improvements Mr. Vere termed them— had been made on the old dwelling-house; but the removal of the dovecot and of the great iron gate on one hand, with the addition of the showy carriages, the sleek horses with plate-harness and the liveried servants that passed and repassed the archway on the other, had often served to excite the regret and jealous bitterness of the last proprietor.

It is an old tradition in Scotland that, if a dovecot is pulled down, the wife of the proprietor usually dies within the year; and though the one at Blairavon was a decided eyesore, its demolition was stigmatized by the old fox-hunter as the act of " an atrocious plebian."

Though modernized internally, so far as possible to suit the requirements of the present day, it was impossible to forget that the old " manor and fortalice " was a place of those days, when, as the old ballad says,—

"A man might then behold,
    At Christmas in each hall,
Good fires to curb the cold,
    And meat for great and small;
The neighbours kindly bidden,
    And all had welcome true;
The poor from gates not chidden
When this old cap was new."

Lennard paused ere he approached the entrance, for the memory of much that his dead father had impressed upon him from childhood—much that he had wisely forgotten while working among practical men at his desk in Liverpool—came welling up now, with something of a choking sensation, as he surveyed the stately old place that had gone from his family for ever.

The rooms in which so many generations of the Blairs had lived with dignity and died with the respect and love of their dependents, where they feasted and roistered, ate and drank, married their daughters with honour, and brought home the daughters of others as wedded brides (whose escutcheons yet were carved on turret and gable), seemed greatly changed now.

The love of the young, the tears of the sorrowing, the pride of some, the wrath of others, had those old walls witnessed for years, as generations succeeded each other, to be gathered at last amid the dust of their predecessors at Inchmachan; and Lennard felt that, though these, with their emotions, had all passed away, there yet lingered in his own heart a mine of bitterness and unavailing regret.

Though silent and lonely enough for eight months of the year since it had passed out of the hands of the old fox-hunting laird (or squire, as those south of the Tweed would style him), Blairavon was instinct with life and gaiety now. Whether it was the result of the grand coal discovery on the estate, Lennard knew not; but he was impressed by an appearance of splendour there, which was not to be found in Vere's villa on the Aigburth-road.

In the drawing-room,—where the shabby, old, oval-backed chairs, chintz-covered sofas, and other furniture of those days of meagre taste, when George III. was king, had given place to marchionesses, couches, and ottomans of damask and velvet; where Brussels' carpets showed their brilliant colours; where, in lieu of the old wax lights, were crystal gasaliers, lit by the produce of the newly-discovered coal-pits; where were stuffed chairs of walnut-wood, of quaint and beautiful design; mirrors that rose from gilded and marble consoles; water-colours by Carrick, Gilbert, and Carl Haarg, all glories which would have filled with wonder the wigged and cuirassed Blairs of other times—in the drawing-room, from which opened now a beautiful conservatory, the shelves whereof were loaded with blooming flowers of singular forms and cabalistic names,—Lennard was received with a smile and blush of pleasure by Hesbia Vere, and with a pretty cordial welcome by her father, and was then presented to the other guests, most of whom were friends then resident with them.

It was with some apparent fuss that Hesbia hastened to introduce Lennard Blair—who was decidedly a distinguished-looking young fellow—to their friends in succession; to Sir Cullender Crowdy, a tall, thin, sallow-visaged, and damp-looking personage; and to Mr. Dabchick, a dapper mannikin of smart, but rather mean appearance. Her cousin, Travice Cheatwood, gave Lennard two fingers only and a greeting the reverse of cordial; and then he was presented to a charming little woman, whom Hesbia named Lady Foster, whose air and singular beauty could not fail to interest him.

" Is not the doctor with you?" asked Hesbia.

" I have not seen him to-day, Miss Vere."

" You are such friends, Mr. Blair, that I never doubted but you and he would come together."

And now, during the pauses that ensue before guests are all arrived or introduced, and duly marshalled—the somewhat dreary interval that so generally precedes a dinner party—Lennard had time to look about him and see who were there.

" Mr. Cheyne and the Misses Cheyne," were announced by a servant in a preposterously showy livery with aiguilettes.

So many more than Hesbia stated were present

now, that Lennard feared he and the Doctor had merely been asked to fill two vacant chairs; but before he could consider this surmise, his hand was warmly shaken by Ranald Cheyne of the Haughs (who, though Lennard knew it not, had many a time kindly paid old Richard Blair's subscription to the West Lothian pack), who then presented him to his " girls," two handsome and blooming blondes, as " the son of his oldest and dearest friend, poor Dick Blair, of Blairavon."

Sir Cullender Crowdy, of Crowdymoudy and that ilk, as he oddly designated himself, though a genuine and undoubted Londoner, was, we have said, a tall, pale, black-haired, and unhealthy looking personage, of some forty-five years, with narrow, stooping shoulders, and long, hairy fingers, with flat tips to them. He inherited no small share of the blood of Judah, though styling himself a baronet of Nova Scotia; his eyes were black as sloes, quick and restless in their expression, and though his hooked nose had been broken, his face somehow always reminded one of a bird of prey.

He did not wear jewellery; but exhibited, rather ostentatiously, a large signet ring, a Scottish amethyst of beautiful hue, whereon was carved the crest of the Crowdy family, with the motto assumed by it in 1707, *Facie Tenus,* which our friend, the Lyon King, assures us can only be Englished as " up to the mark."

In this strange looking personage, of whose title we shall say a little at a future time, Lennard Blair erelong found that he was likely to have a more formidable rival than the adventurer Travice Cheatwood.

Rivalry! as he looked on the wealth and ostentatious luxury around him, how dared he, a poor and almost penniless fellow, think of rivalry; yet he felt almost half assured that the heiress, Hesbia Vere, loved him.

Ten years the senior of Lennard, a " plucked " medical student, a sharp hand at billiards and sharper still at cards, Travice Cheatwood had a very small income, which he eked out in many ways; but his betting-book was his great resource, and the hope of picking up a wife with money was ever before him.

His cousin Hesbia he considered fair game, indeed almost his own peculiar property, and he viewed with emotions little short of savage any interference in that quarter.

Previous to his arrival, Hesbia, whose heart abhorred a vacuum, had been dividing her smiles between Sir Cullender and Mr. Dabchick—flirting desperately with each when the other was not present; though she certainly experienced some difficulty in coquetting with the baronet—a solemn, strange, and reserved man, whose real character she had early found the impossibility of fathoming.

But now the little Edinburgh advocate, Mr. Dalrymple Pennyworth Dabchick—"D. P. Dab," as he was usually called by the small wits of the law courts—had been completely thrown over, and his pique thereat was sobered down into settled disgust; for little Dab thought himself a personage alike of consummate talent and the most colossal public value.

The dislike between Hesbia and the county ladies was quite mutual, so she received the Misses Cheyne with a stately coldness that she should not have displayed in her own house.

Nearly tall in stature, with a rounded queenly figure, Lennard thought Hesbia was looking beautiful. The lily was not whiter or purer than her skin, and her hands and feet were perfect in contour. Her carriage at times was haughty and defiant; and, when excited, she would make her soft-brown eyes flash, and the masses of her crisp chestnut hair move as if they were instinct with life.

Lennard was sighing in the conviction that he, of course, could not be the favoured person who was to lead her as hostess to the dining-room. He was somewhat, relieved, however, when he saw her take the arm of old Doctor Magnus Kirkford, the parish minister; and still more so when she whispered to him behind her fan, just as the gong was beginning to roar in the vestibule,—

"No word yet of your tiresome medical friend; a ploughboy ill with the measles, or some such thing, no doubt. Take in one of the Cheyne girls and sit on my left side, I have so much to say to you."

It was such a whisper and such a glance as Hesbia alone could give, and so poor Lennard's heart began to beat happily, and he was about to address a few words of commonplace to Lady Foster—a pale, little woman, with a clear intellectual type of beauty, a singular sadness and sweetness in her mouth, and deep violet eyes, which had long black lashes, but whose *petite* figure was towered over and outshone by the dashing Hesbia; but ere she could reply to his regret for the absence of her husband, Sir Philip Foster, who had been telegraphed for eastward to Edinburgh, the door was flung open by the tall valet of the calves and aigulettes, who announced in a pompous style,—

"Doctor Francis Feverley!"

Then as the Doctor came forward with a pleasant smile and flushed face, nervous manner, and one of his kid gloves torn, to apologise for being a little late, a faint sound like a gasp escaped Lady Foster, who let both her fan and bouquet fall.

Lennard adroitly picked them up and restored them just as the company began to move off to the dining-room ; then he saw that the camellias of which the bouquet was composed were not more white and waxen in colour than the face of Lady Foster.

Why was this ? Whence the strange emotion ?

CHAPTER XII.

THE DINNER-PARTY.

SUCH entertainments as this one at Blairavon are pretty much alike everywhere, yet among the guests were a few characters or ingredients such as are not to be met with everyday.

All the accessories that wealth and luxury can afford were there; rich viands, various wines, glittering plate and shining crystal, with pomp and servants in shiny liveries, and, oddly enough, not *all* alike; and, from the caviare and curaçoa at the beginning, to the coffee and maraschino at its close, through all its elaborate details of "potages, poissons, relevés, entrées," and so forth, as the gilded and embossed bills of fare had them (to the extreme bother of the parish minister and one or two others), Hesbia's small dinner party was carried out to perfection; and papa Vere, with his red and white clarets, did his part well.

Lennard could detect an elaborate attempt at high *ton* which certainly fell short of the mark, and may have excited the secret ridicule of the servants, who had seen the true metal elsewhere.

He experienced a disappointment, however, at the beginning in not getting the seat next Hesbia; for Miss Cheyne, with whom he had been paired off, lingered to address something to Doctor Feverley, who did not immediately attend or seem to comprehend; and this delay, brief though it was by the subsequent contingency, partially spoiled Lennard's dinner, for the chair on Hesbia's left hand was immediately filled by the dapper Mr. Dabchick.

Travice Cheatwood on that very morning had made a blunt and formal proposal to Hesbia, and had been rejected by her, laughingly however. Cousin Travice was in no way broken-hearted; but though inspired by jealous anger of Lennard and of Crowdy conjunctly and severally, feeling bitterly revengeful, and by many secret circumstances almost desperate, with considerable skill and coolness seemed disposed to revenge himself on Hesbia by engaging in a flirtation with Lady Foster.

This he soon discovered to be an impossibility, as the pale little beauty seemed seriously indisposed, silent, nervous, and incapable of attending to him on the one hand, or to her host on the other; for Mr. Vere could talk only of shares, scrip, and the state of the money market.

Lennard was not without hope that when the ladies retired to the drawing-room, he might have an opportunity (if Hesbia entered the conservatory, or was seated at the piano) of addressing her, and requesting at least an interview—a meeting, somewhere—as a proposal such as he had first fancied seemed then an impossibility; and even with this thought in his head, and the words in which he would give it utterance hovering on his tongue, and while exchanging tender and meaning glances with Hesbia—glances by which they could already understand each other without words—he felt his courage fail.

Amid the wealth that surrounded her, and the stately aspect of the old house, once the home of his father, and now of *hers*, Lennard felt himself a fortune-hunter like Travice Cheatwood, and his proud spirit spurned the false position in which his fate had placed him.

Vere, he knew, had great wealth. He had ships that came and went from the vast docks of Liverpool; argosies whose keels ploughed every sea under the sun. He had a magnificent mansion in the direction of Aigburth, gorgeously furnished, with pictures and bronzes, marble busts and vases, with a retinue of servants; and now he had Blairavon, with more splendours in the way of paintings and

upholstery than the old lairds thereof could have
conjured up without the aid of witchcraft; and more
grooms, gamekeepers, and gardeners, more men and
women servants in and about the place, than were
requisite when Randal Blair entertained the Lords
of the Congregation, or the Regent Murray, when
on his last fatal march to Linlithgow.

Amid the intervals during which the troublesome
silver *entrée* dishes, with cockscombs and mushrooms,
boudoin of lobster, and so forth went round, Lennard
strove to interest himself with the pretty, fair girl
by his side, who, sooth to say, seemed very much
interested in him, for there was a sadness in his
eyes, and an abstraction in his manner, the real
source of which she little suspected; and thus,
while replying to all the graceful nothings she was
saying, he was glancing from time to time at Hesbia,
and listening with weariness to the topics discussed
by those about him.

The sallow, lanky, and black-haired baronet,
though at times affecting to talk " Peerage," slid
more easily and familiarly into a discussion on the
money-market with his host, and seemed to be
much more at home in the disbursements of the
dividends on consols, floating capital, bills, and short
loans, and so forth, than in the works of Sir Robert
Douglas, or Sir Bernard Burke.

The subject of the probable winner of the Derby
was, of course, introduced by Travice Cheatwood,

amid an affectation of talking of the county pack
and races; but no one there seemed disposed to
follow up the topic, not even old Ranald Cheyne
of the Haughs, who knew too much of the speaker
to make even the smallest remark that might be
distorted into a bet. Moreover, he was just then
busy discussing with the minister—who, like most
Scotch divines, farmed his own glebe—the mysteries
of topdressing, subsoil drainage, and planting belts
of firs, of turf dykes, and hedges.

Lennard being a crack shot of the Liverpool Rifle
Corps, Volunteering was next spoken of; but with
great contempt by Mr. Dabchick, as he had not been
made a captain, at least.

At last the ladies rose to retire; and Lennard,
though his eyes followed the stately figure of Hesbia,
as she sailed out of the dining-room, with her long
dress floating behind her, could not fail to detect a
singular mutual glance, one expressive of pain and
sorrow, exchanged by Lady Foster and Doctor
Feverley, as she passed him in her way towards the
door. Strange to say, the Doctor's face was nearly
as pale as her own, and he trembled as her skirt
brushed past him.

"Here lies some hidden secret!" thought
Lennard.

And now the gentlemen began to close in towards
the host, and as the butler replenished the wine
decanters, Travice Cheatwood, who was already a

little elevated, and could not resist the temptation of saying saucy things, began with the doctor and lawyer, simply because they were inoffensive fellows; and certainly he had the peculiar art of dealing in unpleasantry, which could neither be accepted as a jest, nor yet resented as an insult.

"Did you drive over from your shop, Doctor?" he asked.

"I don't keep a shop—if you mean a laboratory, Mr. Cheatwood."

"Well, your diggings, bunk, whatever you call it?"

"I rode. I can't afford to keep a vehicle yet."

"Though a rhubarb-coloured pill-box is useful in its way, you are, perhaps, better without it."

"Why?"

"Few Scotsmen drive well, or are good whips, except," he added deliberately, having heard of Feverley's connection with Jamaica, "except in the West Indies, where they were first-rate drivers of niggers. But the pill-box *is* useful; it may follow as an *empty* compliment at a funeral, when you are doctoring elsewhere," he added, laughing broadly at his own jest.

"Sir, a doctor may very seriously regret the death of a patient," said Feverley, reddening with positive annoyance, yet unwilling to take offence.

"Regret, of course; he is concerned perhaps as much *in* the demise as *at* it."

" How, sir ? "

" It is a loss anyway."

" Pass the decanter," said little Dabchick, who had vainly and nervously made more than one attempt to interrupt Cheatwood, " which wine are you taking, Doctor ? "

" White claret."

" I was once retained in a singular case about white claret."

" Please Dabchick, don't begin to talk law, Scotch law, of all things," interrupted the constitutionally impertinent Cheatwood. " I think that all who go to law are idiots."

" Indeed ! and why so ? " asked Dabchick, looking a little ruffled.

" I am only quoting one of the fraternity in saying so," replied Cheatwood, who having a design to lure Dabchick into a game of billiards (for the lawyer was wearying of ecarté, which they had played every night, and always to his loss), besides, he had no fear of him, so far as Hesbia was concerned, Mr. Dalrymple P. Dabchick being a weak-looking little creature, with sandy hair, sore eyes, and a retroussé nose, with a chin, however, which indicated the most inordinate amount of self-esteem, usually the strongest element which now pervades the provincials of the Bar. " I once heard of an *avocat* of Strasbourg, who, on being taken dangerously ill, sent for a brother of the bag, to make his will, in which he bequeathed to the hospital for the insane, the sum of seventy thousand florins. On his brother-lawyer expressing astonishment at his bequest to idiots,—

"Mon frére," replied the repentant *avocat*, "they are the very persons on whom my ill-gotten gains should be bestowed. From idiots those florins were won, and to idiots they shall return."

While this odd style of conversation went on, Lennard was recalling the repulsion he felt for Cheatwood on that night when, total strangers to each other, they travelled by the express train from Liverpool, and when again he saw him at the church-yard-gate of Inchmachan.

It was, we have said, a peculiarity of Cheatwood's face, that while his mouth was distended by a broad sardonic grin at some of his own supposed witticisms, and showing all his glistening teeth, his eyes remained stolid, unmoved in expression, or having, if anything, a species of cold glare in them.

"Blair, come here beside me," said Mr. Vere, with one of his pleasantest smiles, pointing to the chair which Lady Foster had recently quitted; "I must have a talk with you now that we have an opportunity."

Thus invited, Lennard with alacrity changed his place.

The truth was, that Mr. Vere had a great desire to acquire the little patch of land named Oakwoodlee, "for has not the vineyard of Naboth been always an eyesore to neighbouring potentates?" He disliked the interest that attached to the old family lingering in the neighbourhood, and had his own secret views regarding Lennard Blair; but he knew that the latter set an imaginary, almost superstitious, value upon the retention of the old Jointure House; he had also heard something of the tradition of the Charter Stone, which he wished to see macadamised into metal for the roads, and which he considered as "a piece of old bosh, behind the age, and all that sort of thing;" and he only waited for an opportunity of sounding Lennard as to the sale of the ground, but felt a delicacy in approaching the subject just then.

Times there had been when Mr. Vere was not indisposed to view with favour the intimacy of his daughter and the son of old Blairavon; but now there were secrets in the firm known only to himself which perhaps compelled him to have other views regarding *her*.

"You have looked very dull all the evening, Blair; take another glass of wine, and get up the steam," said Mr. Vere, who, however, could bear with great philosophy the mental or bodily pains of *others*, and whose mouth was compressed, as is usual in those who are much in the habit of restraining such emotions as they have.

"My father was born in this house, my uncle

Lennard, too; and in this house I, too, saw the light, and here my mother died," said Blair, as if to account for his abstraction. "I can remember, as if it were but yesterday, the nodding of the hearse-plumes as the wind stirred the leaves in the avenue when the funeral train went forth, and I sat at that window watching it, and wondering in my little heart what was my loss, why all about me were so sad, and why I was not at her knee. So the old house is, to me, full of the saddest interest, Mr. Vere."

" Of course—of course," replied the other, jingling some silver in his pockets, and thinking there was no use of speaking about Oakwoodlee when Lennard was in this sentimental mood of mind; so, following out his own train of thought, he blundered on in this fashion :—" Your father, worthy man, never could get on well with me, a matter which I now deplore, as it is irreparable."

" Irreparable, indeed !" sighed Lennard.

" As I could not trace back my descent—a thing which no one values nowadays—like those knights and lairds, or what-d'ye-call-'ems of Blairavon, whose queer coats-of-arms are stuck up over all the house, and who very likely could neither sign their names nor earn an honest penny—he thought little of me, indeed ; and never forgave me for being a prosperous and industrious trader, who acquired that which he was throwing to the dogs ; but, pardon me, Blair, and fill your glass; what I say gives you pain, I see."

Lennard did wince with secret annoyance at those remarks which he knew to be perfectly just and true. Then Mr. Vere, who shared some of the angry prejudices of his daughter, added, with what he meant to be a smile,—

"In this rural district, however, Mr. Richard Blair, even in his reduced circumstances was always treated with more respect by the cottars than I. Though I had legally bought Blairavon at its marketable price—bought it with money earned by years of hard and patient industry—the people here view me as a species of intruder; and though I spend thousands in the place, it would be considered good news at the smithy and spirit-shop if I broke my neck in one of the new coalpits, or was found in the pond at Craigellon, like your uncle Lennard."

Lennard intensely disliked the bad taste of all these remarks. He could barely forgive them even in the father of Hesbia, and endeavoured to lead the conversation to the business of the firm, and to some recent correspondence that he had been conducting in Spanish—a language in which he was a proficient —with Don Juan Leonardo & Co., of Vera Cruz; then at once, while the Baronet half-turned his chair and became all attention, Mr. Vere plunged deeply into the matter of imports and exports—flour from America; cotton, sugar, indigo, and spices from the

East Indies; rum, coffee, and tobacco from the
West; and their transactions with the merchants of
Brazil, Chili, and Vera Cruz; in the midst of which
he said,—

"We mean to send you out to Vera Cruz some of
these days, for the double purpose of cementing our
connection with Don Juan, and establishing a branch
of the house there. It will be a most lucrative
agency."

Lennard bowed an assent, but his heart, though
set on future fortune, sank at the thought of leaving
Hesbia behind him, and at that moment there was a
move made by all towards the drawing-room.

While one or two lingered to comment on the
merits of the portrait of a cherry-cheeked girl by
Greuze, and a savage mountain-pass in Calabria, by
Salvator Rosa, Feverley pressed the hand of Lennard,
and said,—

"Would to heaven I had never been invited
here!"

"What on earth is the matter with you, Doctor,
you look positively ill?"

"And ill I am—ill at heart; but, hush! you
remember quizzing me about meeting Lady Foster?"

"Perfectly; the other night, at Oakwoodlee."

"The night I was seized with a—perhaps foolish
fit of confidence.

"Foolish?"

"Pardon me, but my head wanders."

"Well?"

"Oh, Blair! 'upon what slight threads do the events of life turn!' How little could I then imagine that *she*—this Lady Foster—was the Milly Montgomerie of Monkwood? or could you suppose the dark and tender secret that was between us?"

"Do you not confide in me?" asked Lennard, reproachfully, after a pause.

"I believe you to be true as steel."

"But her husband's name was, I thought you told me, Wharton?"

"Changed to Foster for a Cumberland estate, so Dr. Kirkford told me; and he was knighted by the Governor-General at Calcutta as Sir Philip Wharton Foster. I cannot face her again; you know not what we have both endured during the last three hours! I must leave —."

"Not without bidding adieu to Miss Vere; she would never forgive —"

"True, true—poor wretch that I am!"

And they passed on with the other guests.

CHAPTER XIII.

HESBIA'S DRAWING-ROOM.

ON entering the drawing-room, which was lofty, spacious, and magnificently furnished, and lit up, Dr. Feverley looked round with a hasty and haggard glance, and experienced a species of relief on perceiving that Lady Foster was *not* there.

Mr. Vere immediately missed and inquired for her.

"She became indisposed while at dinner, papa," said Hesbia; "did you not perceive how pale she looked?"

"Paleness is her normal colour, I think," said Sir Cullender; "as it is my own, I don't consider it altogether a sign of ill-health, Miss Vere."

"But she is far from well," persisted Hesbia, "and has retired to her own room, where I think the Doctor shouldsee her."

"Not unless she should wish it," said Feverley, with nervous haste; "until she sends for me, I must be excused, my dear Miss Vere, from intruding."

"This is her little boy," continued Hesbia, leading forward a pretty child of some four or five years old, who had been nestling on a hassock by the knee of Mrs. Kirkford, the minister's wife, a kind and motherly old lady, who, together with the Misses Cheyne, had been toying and playing with him, after the manner of ladies with children in general.

"Isn't he a little love, Doctor?" asked one.

A clever observer might have seen how nervously Feverley's lips were quivering, how pale he was, and with how strange a glance he seemed to eye the unconscious child, who looked up to him with eyes of crystal clearness, not dark violet in tint like his mother's, but bright blue like Feverley's own; he had crispy, curly hair, and cheeks that were round and red as winter apples.

"What is your name, darling?" asked the Doctor, as he lifted the child on his knee.

"Franky—little Franky."

"Frank is my name too," said the Doctor, in a somewhat broken voice.

"I am called so from my grandpapa," added the child; "and I am papa's very good boy."

"True, it was his name—I remember," said Feverley, as if speaking to himself.

The boy eyed with wonder, and something of distrust too, this stranger who evinced so much interest in him;—and how was it with the poor Doctor?

As he looked on the little boy's face, and traced there the minute features and the likeness of the mother, all the man's yearning heart seemed to gush forth, and, with something like a sob in his throat, he kissed the boy so tenderly that the latter opened his great blue eyes wider with increasing wonder.

Feverley kept the child on his knee caressingly till his time for bed arrived, and to his nurse—who was sent by mamma—he gave him with a reluctance which caused Hesbia and the young ladies to rally him for his fatherly way; but Travice Cheatwood whispered to them that it was "all acting and professional bosh, by which he hoped to catch mothers of families and lady patients."

Hesbia, who had been in conversation with the clergyman and Mr. Cheyne, now turned from them, and proceeded to open the piano, a task which Lennard hastened to share.

"I am about to play," she whispered.

"What?"

"Oh, anything you please," said she, drawing her gloves hastily off her very white and pretty hands. On her left wrist was a present of which Lennard had begged her acceptance, a bracelet of those beautiful pink-hued Scottish pearls which are now in such high reputation, and which had belonged to his great-grandmother. "You know," she added, "that I can thump out Rossini, Thalberg, and Mendelssohn too; but keep beside me—I am sick of those dreary

country respectabilities, with their weary propriety
and unendurable twaddle; talk to me while I play,
turn the leaves, and make yourself generally useful."

Then running her fingers swiftly over the keys,
Hesbia awoke with spirit the tone of the grand
piano—one of Collard's best repetition-trichords—
as she proceeded to play and converse the while.

" How did you like Miss Cheyne ? "

" Very much."

" Not too much, I hope ! "

" She is a very pleasant, quiet, and lady-like
girl."

" But of a county family—most fearfully county
family—bah ! " added Hesbia, making a crash with
her outspread fingers, while her brown eyes sparkled.
" I hate all such stuck-up people."

" The poor girl gives herself no airs ; she does not
require to do so."

" Is that a hit at me ? "

" Oh, Miss Vere ! " urged Lennard, colouring
with vexation, but saying no more, as he knew this
to be perilous ground with Hesbia ; so he continued
to listen in silence and turn the leaves, for two of
his rivals, Cheatwood and Dabchick, were close by.

" Miss Cheyne has, I know, very pretty hands,"
resumed Hesbia, " and a foot of which she can make
a wonderful use in croquet, when she displays her
instep. Well, I shall be thankful when this

drawing-room is done up in brown holland and lavender, and again abandoned to the spiders for a time."

"Are you already weary of Blairavon?" asked Lennard, with a marked inflection of the voice.

"Weary—I should think so!"

"To me, who have been so long in Liverpool that I was almost forgetting what a mountain was like, this seems strange."

"The country is all very well, but a little bit of it goes a long way with me—Scotland especially. Pardon me, dear Mr. Blair, but I can't help saying so."

The truth was that the county ladies, as Hesbia knew and was wont to say, "understood the whole situation," and valued neither her nor her papa for their reputed wealth. She simply hated them; and knew that at races, meets, and balls they "tolerated her," observed her fast ways, her diamonds, and her dresses with critical eyes and elevated brows, and with manners cold or shy—polite, but never cordial. Even the overdone richness of her toilette—always that of "a girl of the period,"—the perfumes with which every lace and skirt, flounce and flower, were redolent, were commented upon, with her seat on horseback and bearing in the carriage, where she always sat upright and well forward.

The county people she considered simply intolerable!

Yet many there were who admitted that, though
Miss Vere "was vain to her finger-ends," she might
wear the most brilliant colours and dresses beyond
her years, the most wonderful diamonds and jewellery, and yet, singular to say, neither look over-
dressed nor over-decorated, as some girls might have
done.   This arose from the amplitude of her figure,
the purity of her complexion, the brilliance of her
expression, and the general coquettish style of her
undeniable beauty.

She sang many things in good style and with
great good-nature. What they were, Heaven knows;
certainly, Lennard did not, for he was so full of her
and his own thoughts, and especially content with
one feature in the performance—that while linger-
ingly and lovingly turning the leaves, his hand and
hers were always somehow coming in contact.

He was awkward about it, perhaps.

To whisper anything of a private or tender nature
into Hesbia's pretty white ear was impossible then,
for Cheatwood was watching them closely; and
Dabchick, though jealous and disgusted too, was
still disposed to hover about the heiress, who could
only understand the half of what he said, as he
spoke in that wonderful Anglo-Scotch patois peculiar
to his fraternity and the law-courts of the modern
Athens.

Bored by his presence, Hesbia resigned the music-
stool to Miss Cheyne, and led the minister's wife

into her little boudoir, which was a miracle of elegance and luxury—for she was not without taste as well as vanity.

The conversation was pretty general in the room; good digestion seemed to wait on appetite, and while the servants went round with coffee and ices, Mr. Vere was jocose and little Dabchick unusually jolly; even the tall, sallow baronet relaxed his unpleasant visage and taciturn manner; but Travice Cheatwood was vicious. Wine always had a bad effect upon him.

He had been watching the scene at the piano, and thought he discovered a silent but secret understanding between Hesbia and Lennard Blair, on whom he now resolved to fasten, and whom he arrested at the door of the boudoir, whither our hero was about to follow Hesbia.

In his deep and angry suspicions of Lennard, the cousin was anxious to discover the real state of matters between him and Hesbia; but though a cunning he was a blundering fellow, and knew not how to go about it. Somehow, impertinence came more naturally to him than suavity, and after luring Lennard to a long and stately corridor (which lay between the drawing and dining-rooms) on pretence of looking at a picture,—

"It is an absurd, even ugly, looking place, this house of Blairavon," said he; "I wonder how the governor ever came to buy it."

"Absurd?" queried Lennard, reddening; "ugly, do you say?"

"Pardon me—by Jove! I forgot that the old place once belonged to your family," he replied, sneeringly.

"It was my father's and his forefathers', for centuries, and is very ancient."

"Well, a place may be old and yet be unsightly or absurd, just as a man may be old and disreputable, or a spendthrift."

"I don't see the parallel," said Lennard, abruptly turning on his heel, and re-entering the drawing-room.

"Dry, proud snob!" muttered Cheatwood, savagely, and with a dangerous gleam in his eye; "but I'll take the wind out of your sails yet, my fine fellow—our junior partner, as you think yourself. By Jove, if you only knew as much of old Vere as I do, you might be less easy in your mind."

Cheatwood, however, had no desire to quarrel outwardly with Blair; he knew that the young man had some loose cash, to share which over cards would be very convenient; then there was the secret in regard to Hesbia, which he wished to learn; so he became more suave in his manner, and artfully contrived to get himself included in an invitation to a dinner which Lennard was giving to the Doctor and Dabchick, "just to come over in a friendly way and take their lamb and green peas with him at Oakwoodlee about six to-morrow."

"Thanks; I am your man," said Travice," "do we play ccarté?"

"A little," said Lennard.

"Then we shall have a game to-morrow night, or cut in for a quiet rubber, eh?"

"With pleasure," said Lennard : but Dabchick, who had played a good deal with Mr. Cheatwood of late, made a faint response ; and that gentleman, feeling assured that the morrow would be a lucrative day, went gaily through the drawing-room into the conservatory where Hesbia was good-naturedly culling a nosegay for old Mrs. Magnus Kirkford, before the good lady set out for the manse.

Lennard, who was still speaking to Feverley, did not observe where Cheatwood had gone; he only knew that Hesbia was busy among the shelves of brilliant exotics, and went there also, for the purpose of attempting to interest her by the double announcement that he was soon to start for Liverpool, and afterwards, for a long and indefinite time, to Vera Cruz; and he was fully intending to make some allusion to a more defined and tender form of friendship; but this intention, like his feelings, received a shock—a check, on hearing nothing less than a proposal made to her by another, and his unintentional eavesdropping came about in the following manner :—

CHAPTER XIV.

A PROPOSAL.

THE conservatory was spacious, with a great pyramidal stand, or shelved partition in the centre; and while passing round this barrier, which intervened between him and Hesbia, Lennard, to his extreme annoyance, was joined by his father's old friend, Mr. Cheyne, who was a great florist, and was always pottering about bulbs, cucumber beds, melon frames, and so forth. Unfortunately, being rather deaf, he was quite unaware of the presence of others in the conservatory, so he at once engaged Lennard in a discourse upon hot-air apparatus and exotics with mysterious names and properties; but this did not prevent the unlucky lover, whose ears were quickened by apprehension, from hearing Hesbia and Travice Cheatwood in close conversation on the other side of the great flower-stand.

"You remember our little confab, Hesbia?" asked Cheatwood.

I   M

"When? we have so many confabs, as you call them."

"And disputes, too; but I mean this morning."

"Well; but don't recur to it, please."

"And why not?"

"It is useless to refer to your magnificent proposal."

"Sneering again, and thereby adding pain——"

"Pain!" echoed Hesbia, laughing; "now don't be a fool, Travice; once and for all, I cannot and will not have you."

"Will not, and cannot! Are you in earnest, or is this some of your flirting nonsense?"

"I am in stern earnest," she said, laughing again, and burying her pink nostrils into the bouquet she was arranging with great taste and skill.

"Laughed at, am I?" continued Travice, grinding his teeth. "Well, I came down to this outlandish hole, and have loafed about it on a precious fool's errand."

"Not entirely so, if papa gave you some days ago the cheque for £400, which you spoke of this morning, to show me how high you stood in his favour."

Travice Cheatwood changed colour painfully, for the document referred to had undergone some remarkable changes in his hands.

"I am sure, also," added Hesbia, "that you win money from all our friends."

"I have won £60 from the baronet and Dabchick at billiards, and done that soft snob of a Doctor into the odds on 'Traviata' at the Epsom, though the poor fool knows nothing about it—don't think he even knows where Epsom is, though I suppose he has heard of the salts so named. But it is hard to be treated thus by you, Hesbia, after enduring your baronet, Dabchick, old Kirkford, and that set to the last stage of boredom."

"Sweet cousin, you are very polite!" said she, curtseying.

"I'll not take to Tennyson and a cigar for breakfast, or to Byron and moonlight for supper, at all events," he replied, while eyeing her malevolently.

"You would require to turn over a new leaf to suit me, Travice, dear," said Hesbia, willing to coquette a little with him still.

"I always mean to do so."

"To-morrow, no doubt?"

"Yes, but I can never overtake to-morrow."

"Why?" continued Hesbia, banteringly.

"Because it is always twelve hours ahead. Your governor——"

"Say 'papa.' I am shocked by your slang, Travice."

"Well, your papa makes money by the bushel, the old name and spirit of Cheatwood are still in the firm; and why should not I benefit thereby?"

" Your father's interest was bought ; and you have always been a bad boy."

Cheatwood uttered an oath.

" Come, now, Travice, let me pass to the drawing-room, and don't be absurd, or make a fool of yourself by growing angry."

" If any other person is the means of making a fool of me by —— (and with flashing eyes and a pallid visage, he swore again, looking as ruffianly as his speech imported) I'll make cold meat of him, and send him to old Fireworks before his time ! "

Hesbia shrugged her smooth shoulders, and said disdainfully,—

" Don't indulge in tall talk."

" Who is using slang now ? "

" Melodramatic threats are intensely absurd, and there are rural police even in Scotland. You must have seen them, cousin—big six-foot fellows, in sham military uniforms, with thistles and St. Andrew's crosses on their felt helmets. They are vulgarly muscular and unpleasant-looking men."

Thus bantered, Cheatwood withdrew scowling, and in his confusion, or irritation, stumbled without apology against the pale and shark-eyed baronet, who was lingering at the conservatory door.

Had he been aware of what was going on ? Anyway he was looking as dark as if " things were wrong in Mincing- or Mark-lane—or the devil was upon 'Change."

The night was too far advanced now to afford Lennard time for the opportunity so earnestly sought.

Mr. Cheyne and his daughter drove off, taking the clergyman and his wife in their carriage, as the manse of Blairavon stood on the way to the Haughs. Doctor Feverley now appeared hat in hand, and Lennard, who had no excuse for lingering, prepared to depart.

Hesbia bade him adieu cordially and with much *empressement,* slyly returning the pressure of his fingers with her right hand, while the left, which was placed behind her, we are sorry to add, she permitted Cheatwood to kiss, when he pretended to stoop for a fallen flower.

Crowdy's quick, small eyes saw the whole affair, though Lennard did not ; and with the memory of that coquettish pressure of his hand, and of the soft, tender smile of two beautiful brown eyes, he walked homeward almost a happy man, with his friend the Doctor.

The latter was mounted, and rode slowly by his side buried in thought.

The night was beautiful, the air calm and soft, not a leaf was stirring in the woods of Blairavon, the green hills stood clearly defined in the moonlight on one hand, on the other Lennard could see the blue sky reddened by the glare from the engines by which those mines of wealth, the coal-pits, were worked night and day by double gangs of men— wealth, the loss of which had broken his father's heart.

The Vere " set " was not a very distinguished one; such was Lennard Blair's decided conviction, and he deplored it. Lady Foster was certainly irre- proachable in bearing, manner, and appearance; but the baronet with the odd name, Sir Cullender Crowdy, seemed to be a man there was no fathom- ing, and he resolved to question Dabchick closely about him on the morrow, for Dabchick knew some- thing of everybody or of everybody's affairs.

" It was a great relief to me, Blair, when I found that Lady Foster was *not* in the drawing-room on our return to it," said the Doctor, letting his reins drop on the horse's mane. " I could not again trust myself in her presence. There is more than the mere sentiment of a boyish first love in this, for I am no longer a boy nor she a girl. I believe in this strong and tender love, though not that it either breaks the heart or completely blights a life—"

"Except in novels," said Lennard.

" Novels of course—yet it has cast a shadow on my days."

After a pause,

"I would to God, Blair, I had not met her again—had not looked upon her face!" exclaimed

Feverley in a broken voice; "and then there is her old and palsied husband too—tottering on the verge of eternity."

"It was lucky we escaped him, I think," said Lennard, scarcely knowing what to say.

"My love for Milly has flamed up anew; but it is as the flame of the lamp which the ancients left with their dead—a light I dare not show, dare not acknowledge even to myself—a flame hidden in a tomb!"

And much more did the poor Doctor say and rhapsodise to describe his emotions, till Lennard, to change the subject, said,

"And now that you have seen him, Feverley, what do you think of my rival?"

"Which?"

"The deuce—have I *two?*"

"Well, the lanky baronet with the broken nose and Jewish looking eyes watched you and Miss Vere the whole evening like a lynx. Of course she is a prize that many will contend for; but you refer to Mr. Cheatwood."

"Yes," said Lennard curtly, with an air of annoyance.

"I think he is 'a dog in forehead, and at heart a deer'—or worse, a wolf rather. If Gall and Spurzheim knew anything of their trade, I may say that fellow's head and face should hang him!" said Doctor Feverley.

"Rivalry apart, though the features are good, I cannot help agreeing with you, Doctor, and think that Lavater would do so too."

"But he dines with us at Oakwoodlee to-morrow, does he not?"

"I had no desire to invite him; but he was standing near when I asked you, and politeness—"

"Of course; but I must beware of him; he has entangled me—how I cannot tell—in a bet on an English race, a matter of which I am as ignorant as of what Professor Smyth saw in the Great Pyramid. That Cheatwood has views with regard to his cousin there cannot be a doubt, and that he seems a reckless — even dangerous character too. But that baronet—"

"Oh, Feverley, the man is perfectly hideous!"

"He has a title; Mr. Vere knows its value; the baronet is a man, I hear, well known on 'Change, thoughwhat his line of business I never could precisely learn; and I know enough of Mr. Vere to see that Mammon is the god of his idolatry."

They proceeded in silence for a time, and the lights of Blairavon were hidden among the copsewood now. Following up the last train of thought, Feverley said,—

"By the late melancholy event at home, your income will of course be increased, Blair."

"My father left many debts; but these and all expenses paid, by letting the shootings and a few acres of grass and so forth, I shall have £200 yearly—and then there is a salary or share in the business at Liverpool."

"All this would be wealth to me; such are things by comparison."

"Still all are little enough to offer for Miss Vere's acceptance."

"Yet how pleasant it is to put one's foot upon a piece of land—even an acre or two—and feel that it is one's *own*."

"True," said Lennard thoughtfully as he looked over the fertile miles of meadow and green-growing corn that should have been his, stretching away in the moonlight to the very base of the hills; but now they had reached the little wicket of the pathway that led to Oakwoodlee, the roughcast façade of which shone white amid its dark grove of Scottish pines. There the friends parted, and the Doctor galloped off towards his little cottage in the hamlet.

CHAPTER XV.

BUSINESS.

WHILE this conversation was going on between Lennard and Feverley in the noonlight, a mile or so from Blairavon, another was being maintained on the subject of Hesbia by Mr. Vere and Sir Cullender, as they lingered over their cigars and a glass of madeira, in the smoking-room, where the gas-lights were subdued in the gilt brackets that projected from the wall, and where, through the open windows, the moonlight and the soft atmosphere of the summer night stole pleasantly in together.

The decorations of this room were very simple. The walls were of olive-green tint, and the carpet of cocoa-nut matting; divans and easy chairs of various kinds were there, with spittoons of elegant patterns and boxes of cigars, while on the walls were a few racing and hunting pictures, which whilom had belonged to old Mr. Richard Blair.

Mr. Cheatwood and Mr. Dabchick were in the billiard-room at the other end of the corridor.

Indeed all the leisure moments of the former gentleman were spent in that apartment, practising cannons and wonderful. strokes, or in the study of his betting-book and his chances on the Newmarket Craven meeting, the Catterick Bridge races, and so forth; in noting horses struck out of their engage-ments, arrivals, entries for selling, and other sporting news; and this branch of study on " coming events " he usually pursued with knitted brows and bitten nails, or strange exclamations, as hope or perplexity influenced him.

Left to themselves for a half-hour or so, Mr. Vere and the baronet were seated each under a gas bracket, by means of which position each thought he could watch the play of the other's features while he kept his own concealed; for the conversation ran chiefly on Hesbia and the baronet's presents and attentions to that young lady—attentions which he frankly admitted he had been paying, and she had been receiving with apparent good grace.

Vere was angling to secure the baronet for a son-in-law; while the latter was extremely curious to know how money matters stood, or might stand in the future.

" You are young-looking, Sir Cullender—without a grey hair," remarked Mr. Vere during a pause.

" Still I am past five-and-forty—you flatter me."

" A period not too old for love-making, I hope."

" For romantic love-making certainly," said the

baronet, his quick, small eyes twinkling hideously;
"but that is a commodity in which we business men
—we men of the world, Mr. Vere, are not wont to
traffic."

"No time for it—eh, Sir Cullender? Your title
is recommendation enough to any young girl," said
Vere.

The baronet gave an uneasy smile.

"In what part of Scotland did the estates of
your family lie?"

"In the north."

"And they were lost, you say?"

"In some of the civil wars. Since then we have
resided in England—taken root in London, in
fact."

"And to better purpose, no doubt. At five-and-
forty it is not too old, I hope, to admire beauty and
enjoy all the pleasures of life, which are in the flush
in some measure."

"Your daughter, Miss Vere, is, I admit,
charming," said the baronet; "and she has dazzled
me greatly; but she seems to dazzle all, especially
that young fellow Blair."

"How?" asked Mr. Vere, angrily.

"His gaze was never off her to-night."

"Blair—pshaw! They are good friends, that is
all. He is in my counting-room, and —and
believes himself to have a share in the firm."

An expression of intelligence and intense cunning

played for a moment over the sallow features of Sir Cullender, as he echoed the word "Believes?"

"Yes—yes," replied Mr. Vere, with a careless air, while rattling his pocketfuls of loose silver; "a thousand or two sunk with us—that is all. The reason that I tolerate him here is, that I want to get his patch of land called Oakwoodlee into my own hands —it is a nuisance having it thrust like a wedge into the heart of my estate—and then I shall find an excuse for despatching him to South America—say Vera Cruz."

Mr. Vere said all this very fast, and endeavouring to look, what he wished to be thought—a god in the business-world of Liverpool.

"But to return to Hesbia," he resumed, after a pause; "You have means, Sir Cullender—though, as you admitted to me a few days ago, not much."

"True, Mr. Vere; but I have my title."

Mr. Vere coughed — dubiously, it might have sounded to some; and certainly it did so to the large, projecting ears of the baronet, whose sloe-black eyes gave him an angry and uneasy glance, while he sharply puffed his cigar.

"And with Hesbia as your wife—"

"Without more means than I possess," said the other, coming to the point at once, "a wife is a luxury I cannot well afford, and, accustomed as Miss Vere has been, to all that wealth could give her——; "

"She shall have Blairavon at my death; and if you cast your lot with us, your title being added to the name of the firm—"

"Ah—you think it would sound well?"

"And perhaps prove a mine of gold to us; doubtless you must have found its value in your own business in London?"

"Then there is your nephew, Mr. Cheatwood," said Sir Cullender, abruptly changing the subject.

"A worthless fellow, I am sorry to say. He has no share whatever in the firm, and he is not deserving of consideration. Your business—"

"It is as a dangler after Miss Vere I mean," persisted the baronet, who always with some nervousness evaded any questions about his "business." Perhaps he was ashamed of it, as a man of title and family.

"Travice is a dangler who will not be long here, and I repeat that he is not worth considering."

"But this lad Blair is," rejoined the other, half sulkily.

"Well, perhaps, Hesbia has some friendship for him."

"Then his presence I will not tolerate," said the baronet, who seemed determined to make the most of this; "she wears a valuable bracelet of pearls, which he gave her."

"The young man is frequently my guest and her escort, when we are at home. The gift was openly given, and is openly worn, so I don't put so much weight upon that matter——"

"As he may do, Mr. Vere."

"Since the thing annoys you, Sir Cullender, I shall desire Hesbia to restore it to the donor."

"By no means; that would be attaching, perhaps, too much importance to the gift."

"You have seen her playfulness; she is still a species of child."

"At her years a child, Mr. Vere?"

"Amid the splendour your wealth and business can give her, in a year or so, she will look back on all this philandering and coquetting——"

"With regret or shame, perhaps; but meantime it won't suit me," said the baronet, with the air of annoyance which he always adopted when his mysterious business was alluded to; and this odd bearing had usually the effect of reducing Mr. Vere to silence, or perhaps it set him thinking.

"You have not yet, I believe, addressed my daughter formally?"

"I have not had a proper opportunity, and now that Mr. Blair——"

"Blair returns to Liverpool in three days," said Mr. Vere, with some asperity. "I have a little part to play with him, wishing, as you know, to possess that place named Oakwoodlee; then the whole place shall be settled on Hesbia, by a trust deed of disposition, divesting myself of it in her favour, while solvent; we never know what may occur in trade and in the money market nowadays."

"Then buy up Oakwoodlee."

"Blair won't sell it readily, I fear."

"Won't?"

"Morever, the money-market is pretty tight just now; so I shall give him in exchange for his interest in the place a share to its full value in our business Liverpool. Another time then, Sir Cullender, we shall go thoroughly into these matters—perhaps when I go up with you to London, where you must be equally frank with me in the details of your plans and exchequer, and the close of the year may see my daughter Lady Crowdy."

More might have passed, but Travice Cheatwood now dropped in to smoke a cigar, as he said, " before going to roost;" and as he stroked his fair moustache and smiled complacently to himself, neither Mr. Vere nor his intended son-in-law could have suspected that he had heard more of their plans and wishes than they could have desired, for Travice Cheatwood never entered a room hurriedly.

CHAPTER XVI.

A QUARTETTE.

THE unwonted occasion of guests coming to Oak-woodlee put the two faithful old servants composing the household of Lennard on their metal. Steinie went forth with his rod, and was successful in landing a fine salmon grilse, seven pounds in weight. The recesses of the wine-binns were searched; a bottle or two of the fine old Madeira were put in the sun to air, and those of some other wine in the bucket of the deep draw-well to cool, while Elsie, with sleeves rolled up, made the most wonderful pastry, and put fowls to the spit, being careful to select as one, in the old Scottish fashion, the plump hen that sat next the cock on the roost.

Entrées, ices, camellias, champagne, and maraschino there were none in Oakwoodlee; but from his little garden Steinie produced the sweetest of green peas, the most mealy of young potatoes, luscious and tender esculents of various kinds, with strawberries to the rich cream produced by Elsie's favourite "crummie." So nature nobly supplied all that was wanting in art or decoration.

Doctor Feverley arrived first, a few minutes before six o'clock, looking a little paler than he had done on the preceding evening.

"I have had a little adventure since last night, Blair," said he.

"Not an unpleasant one, I hope?"

"This morning, about daybreak, a mounted servant came from Blairavon in haste, stating that the Lady Foster was seriously indisposed, and that Miss Vere requested me to see her immediately. That no time might be lost, I took the groom's horse, and with intense reluctance and regret, mingled with a painful longing and curiosity, galloped over to the manor-house, where I was informed that the lady declined to see me."

"Declined!"

"Yes, with many apologies. I could not reprehend her. It all passed for the whim—the sudden caprice of a fine lady. How little could Miss Vere, while pleading her excuses for disturbing me at so untimeous an hour, have surmised the real state of matters, as she stood smiling and bowing to me in the most becoming of morning dresses, edged at the sleeves and bosom with soft white lace, and her brown hair knotted hastily back over two very pretty cars, imparting to her brilliant beauty that gala look which is so characteristic of her. There is, says a writer, 'a class of women who are born to be either pets or victims,' and poor Milly has been both— a sacrifice at the two altars of Mammon and Misfortune. When I think of the wreck of her young heart, my own seems to fill with tears."

"Cheer up, Feverley. Sir Philip is an old fellow, palsied and all that; take time, she may be a widow one of these days." Lennard Blair felt himself on the point of making some such rantipole speech as this, when, with all the rapidity of thought, he checked it, and blushed at his own bad taste. He was silent, but after a time said,—

"Come, Feverley, we shall have but a dull, little party if you begin thus. There are wines on the table and brandy on the sideboard."

But the Doctor, abstemious like his profession in general, declined both before dinner.

Lady Foster, on the plea that Sir Philip was unwell at Monkwood Moat, was leaving Blairavon for Edinburgh at that very hour. Poor Feverley was ignorant of this; and for several subsequent days spent much of his spare time in hovering about the vicinity of the avenue and lawn, in the hope of once again seeing the little boy with his nurse.

The Doctor was full of this new, or rather old, subject, and continued to relate to Lennard how, during the long and tedious dinner at Blairavon, he had watched her, and observed what others did not

—her eyes cast down or looking round at times with
a startled, wild, or desolate expression; at others,
wistful and dreary; and how she would anon force
a well-bred smile, and make attempts to reply or
attend to the little nothings that were said around
her; and how she seemed so girlish in appearance,
that she could scarcely be thought the mother of her
son, and so forth.

In the midst of these remarks, the hard, shrewd
Scotch face of Steinic Hislop—who had donned his
old and carefully brushed livery-coat—appeared at
the door with his mouth and eyes all puckered by a
broad grin, as he announced two names which
seemed to tickle his fancy,—

"Mr. Dalrymple Pennyworth Dabchick and Mr.
Cheatwood."

These gentlemen entered, the former attired in
accurate evening dress, and the latter in his shooting-
jacket; and then the usual greetings and meaningless
discussion of the weather ensued prior to dinner.

Dabchick, as a very soured Scottish essayist has
it, was exactly one of those "barristers of provincial
education and very mediocre parts—men who, in
England, *might* become Recorders or County Court
Judges, but who affect to lead a party in Scotland,
because Scotland has become a province, whose
affairs are no longer in the hands of its aristocracy
(all the better surely for Scotland!) and whose
ablest men emigrate if they can."

With all his professional vanity and self-esteem, which were inordinate, in the air of Mr. Dabchick among strangers there seemed something of always deferring—of perpetual apology—of " booing," as Sir Pertinax would call it; but this was simply the result of his training.

Cheatwood had early discovered one very weak point in the character of Dabchick,—an extreme touchiness on the subject of Scottish law; so, whenever they played, he contrived to make the little barrister nervous, furious, and even confused by vulgar ridicule of it, for his own acquisitive ends.

If Lennard's dinner, in style and equipage was a very different affair from the one at Blairavon yesterday, there was a homely, snug, old-fashioned air about it, and the mode in which it was served, that made it a very pleasant repast, though Lennard's eye would wander at times to a certaiu empty elbow chair, and to a corner where an old ivory-handled cane was standing just where his father had last placed it.

An old and wall-eyed otter terrier, named "Don," long his father's faithful friend, now nestled by Lennard's chair, expectant of an occasional morsel.

Even while sharing his hospitality with Cheatwood, it was occasionally with difficulty that Lennard could preserve an unruffled aspect, when the constitutional and irrepressible impertinence of that personage became apparent.

"And you go back to Liverpool in three days, Blair?" he observed, while taking more peas to his salmon.

"In three days at furthest—back to business once more."

"Ah! you are just one of those sort of fellows who always go ahead."

"I hope so—you flatter me."

"No, I don't—not a bit; for I never knew one of your inf—— your countrymen otherwise. They get into the right groove somehow, and then go forward. You'll be head of the house of Vere, Cheatwood and Co. some of these fine days, while I may enlist or hang myself—it's the *line* anyway."

"Steinie, assist Mr. Cheatwood to wine," said Lennard, colouring a little.

"You are silent, Doctor—of what are you thinking?" asked Travice.

"Of the ease and contentment that must be often brought by wealth, and are so seldom the lot of mere work and poverty."

"True; if one had a little tin, this Vale of Tears —as that old psalm-singing muff of a minister called the world yesterday—would be a very jolly place. It is the deuce to be like me, with small means and no profession, and to be constantly trying to make a pleasant circle."

"Of what—acquaintances?"

"No—by coaxing the two ends of my income to

meet; but by no human ingenuity, of mine at least, can that monetary problem be solved."

"Get a rich wife," suggested Mr. Dabchick, who was constantly on the outlook for such an investment of his own dapper person.

"A widow, or an amatory spinster of forty, if either had money, would suit me admirably; but I have never the luck to meet them."

Lennard positively hated Travice Cheatwood; but then, as Hesbia's cousin, he was disposed to conciliate and, as her rejected lover, he could afford to pity him. Still, as the evening stole on, almost every remark made by Travice jarred on Lennard's nerves, on his pet fancies or secret thoughts, and as he imbibed the fine old heady Madeira, his guest's general disposition was not improved. As he lay back in his chair and surveyed the fine and fertile landscape that stretched away beyond the grove of pines and the old Charter Stone,—

"When Sir Bernard Burke, the Ulster King-at-Arms, writes a history of the *unlanded* gentry, I hope he will not forget me," said Travice. "It is a fine thing to own a lump of land; people speak of the wealth of Vere and Cheatwood; but I expect, by Jove, that uncle's best and most lasting mines of wealth are those pits at—what's the absurd name of the place — Kaims of Mains, or Mains of Kaims?"

"Meaning literally 'the field of the camp.' A

Roman camp stood there in the days of Julius Agricola," observed Feverley.

"Now, I should not wonder but that uncle had a shrewd notion of coal being there before he bought the estate from your father, Blair."

"I think that scarcely possible, Mr. Cheatwood."

"Ah—you don't know him as I do."

"You are of a singularly suspicious nature," said Feverley, smiling.

"And perhaps with reason."

"Why?"

"I don't know; but I believe that very few things are done in this world for the causes assigned to them; and you, Dabchick, as a lawyer, must know that deuced well. Under the surface of life lies a stratum of concealed thought which no man can see in his neighbour."

"Of course, that may be," assented Doctor Feverley.

"Every man plays a double game in this world— a secret and an open one; and it is fools alone who let others see the cards they hold."

"A dark and unpleasant distrust this, surely?" said Lennard.

"Unpleasant?"

"Yes—for yourself."

"But useful; I have lived a little longer than you, Blair, in this nothing-for-nothing world, and perhaps know its crooked ways better—that is all."

Whatever was the train of angry thoughts that passed through the cynical and mischievous mind of Cheatwood, his companions could only see that there was a cruel and malevolent expression on his thin lips and in his cold, cunning eye, as Feverley afterwards said, "A most hateful aspect to read in the face of a man who had the most part of life yet before him."

"There may be some truth in what you say," said Lennard, "yet I have been struck by a writer who remarks, 'How little do we know of the hearts of others, and how readily do we prate about seeing through a man, when, in truth, what we see is but a surface, and the image conveyed to our mind but the reflection of *ourselves*.' You do not, then, think much of the world at large?" added Lennard, laughing.

"Neither then nor now," was the surly rejoinder; "and I don't expect much from its candour or generosity."

"Come, come, Cheatwood," exclaimed Lennard, pushing the decanters towards the speaker, "you are turning quite a cynic; fill your glass, and be jolly. Life I know to be a game of leapfrog at best."

"Yes," responded Cheatwood, his large tongue rendering his voice still more displeasing as his

secret irritation grew upon him; "but I shall never,
if I can help it, be the one who stoops his back to
his fellows." And, with a forced laugh, he filled his
glass and held it between him and the light of the
setting sun to test the brilliant hue of the wine.
Then, though all unconscious of it, his next remark
drew upon him a very deliberate scowl from Steinie
Hislop, who, having removed the cloth, was reple-
nishing the wine-decanters. "By the way, Blair,
I'd have that great upright block, which looks very
like as if it had been stolen from Stonehenge—the
Charter Stone, I think you call it,—blown up or
broken down for road metal."

"For what reason?"

"Because it must stand right in the way of the
plough."

"We have never ploughed that piece of land."

"Others may, some day; moreover, it is most unsightly—positively hideous!"

"Well—it may only be the association of ideas or
custom, but it does not seem so to me. Those great
Druidical monoliths that stand here and there all
over the land are calculated to inspire the reflective
mind with many solemn thoughts of all the mighty
changes and the generations of men they have sur-
vived. Moreover," added Lennard, with a little
laugh and almost with a blush, as if ashamed of the
admission to a sneerer, "through an old tradition,
we believed it to be inseparably connected with our

existence as a family, so much so, that an ancestor
of mine was once very nearly adopting it as a crest,
in lieu of the stag's head *caboshed.*"

" Bosh, indeed ! " exclaimed Cheatwood, with the
first genuine laugh he had enjoyed that evening;
" when that far-travelled individual, ' the intelligent
foreigner,' or the ' New Zealander,' to whom the
newspaper snobs always appeal or refer, comes this
way, won't they stare a bit to see such things believed in ——"

" Nay—talked about."

" Well—even talked about, in these days of progress. To be practical men, as you think your-
selves, you Scotsmen are sometimes very sentimental
donkeys, with many sympathies and superstitions
that are all of a pre-railway age. But now, that
dinner is over and wine on the table, suppose we cut
in for a quiet little rubber at whist—crown points,
say ? "

" Impossible for me," said Feverley, looking at
his watch; "I beg your pardon, Blair; but I'm
almost due at the village—have a patient to see;
I shall be back within an hour—you'll hold me
excused."

" Certainly, my dear fellow—return as soon as
you can, and light a cigar ere you go; there are
some prime Havannahs in that box."

The Doctor retired, with a covert glance at Lennard to be wary in his play.

"Now, Mr. Dabchick," said Lennard, "as playing whist with a dummy is always slow work, I shall
smoke a cigar alone, while you and Mr. Cheatwood
take to cards if you choose."

"All right," replied Cheatwood, "only I hate to
play while an idler looks on. (He had his own
private reasons for this strange dislike!) But now,
Dab, to give you a chance of revenge, suppose we
cut in for écarté?"

"What do you mean by revenge?" stammered
Mr. Dabchick.

"You know that I have your I.O.U. for a cool
fifty pounds — perhaps you may win it back
again."

Poor Dabchick gave a sickly smile; he could but
ill afford to take up that obnoxious paper, and had,
he feared, but a slender chance of regaining it from
such a sharp player as Travice Cheatwood; so a cold
perspiration came over him. How many pages of
his guinea-per-column work for the local papers,
with his other perquisite, the sale at half-price to
the libraries of the London books wasted for provincial reviews—a trick of the country press—would
be required to cover that sum; for he was one of
the three hundred and fifty unbriefed of his fraternity, so the consideration was a serious one!

A hectic crossed his face, and he was about to
give his place to Lennard, but, somehow, before he
knew how it all came about, he found himself oppo-

site the inexorable Cheatwood at a little side-table;
while Lennard, thinking of how he could contrive
to have an interview with Hesbia on the morrow,
sat in a window apart from them, solely intent, apparently, on rolling up and smoking a succession of
tiny cigarettes.

CHAPTER XVII.

ÉCARTE.

ENTIRELY anxious to win, Cheatwood played
with great caution, and with his glass stuck
in his eye. He had made up what he conceived to
be a sure and lucrative book on both the Derby and
the Oaks, and in both instances had he lost ! Hence
the origin of that bitterness of spirit which he had
displayed during dinner. Money he must make
now at all hazards, and he valued Blair, Feverley,
and Dabchick at—not much—but about fifty pounds
each at an average. More he did not expect to get
out of them by any ingenuity.

Having sufficient food for his own thoughts,
Lennard sat smoking in the open window, gazing
out on the beautiful landscape that stretched away
towards the base of the green Pentlands, steeped
in the splendour of sunset, and for a time he gave
no heed to the two players, till the odd way in
which they were managing this very rooking game
attracted his attention. Dabchick was considerably

flushed or pale by turns. He had already lost
several games and as many pounds; aud found
himself further than ever from recovering that
obnoxious I O U.

Travice Cheatwood was always overbearing and
insolent, even to equals; so that to subordinates or
inferiors his bearing was singularly offensive. Dabchick he viewed as a species of "muff," and thus made
him a regular butt, but always in an undertoned
way. Perhaps it was that he had a bad hand, or
that Cheatwood had contrived to sting him, by
vulgar banter, on their favourite subject of discussion—the comparative merits of the laws of the two
countries; but when Lennard turned to the card-
table, the game was being conducted in this
fashion :—

"I won't exchange my cards this time, Dab, old
boy," said Cheatwood.

"Then I score double for the tricks."

"Of course; mild play this; but as I was saying
about your Scotch law—only look at its phrases now !
How does the panel appear when the diet against
him is deserted *simpliciter?* very queer, I suppose ?"

"What do you call a puisne judge, and how does
he look when he is sitting in Error?" retorted
Dabchick.

"How the deuce should I know? I'm not a
lawyer, thank God ! What do *you* mean by a double-
gowned senator of the college of justice, and how

does *he* look when he takes a case to avizandum—
wherever that may be?"

" You surely don't know Latin, sir!".

" Nor you Norman French!"

" No—nor Choctaw nor Cherokee—where would
be the use? I mark the king—the card is in your
hand—*Je propose.*"

" Then what do you Scotch lawyers mean
by——?"

" Don't argue with me, please," urged Dabchick,
against whom game after game went dead and
surely, for his adversary could talk away on any
subject, and yet be all the while intent on his points
and counters; " bother Scotland and her laws! I
don't set up for a patriot,—none of us do."

" It doesn't pay you Scotch legal prigs to be so;
but some day I hope you will get rid of your mediæval
law jargon."

" I don't know what you call jargon," replied
Dabchick, becoming seriously ruffled; " but I consider the legal phraseology of our courts quite
as classical and comprehensive as any used in the
south; to wit, what on earth is meant by such terms
as prochein amy, trover, replevin, formedon, nc
unques, and accouple?"

" Words to raise the wind, if not the devil,
certainly," said Lennard, thinking it time to interfere, and laughing at the odd manner in which they
were managing their game of écarté.

" I have won that trick, Dab."

" Play another card, please — this is our last game, remember."

The tricks were rapidly played out, and when Dabchick rose from the table he was minus twenty pounds. This was not a great sum; but as things are comparative, when added to the I O U it was sufficient to render Dabchick wretched.

As the game had gone on, the reason why Travice Cheatwood " hated to play " with an idler by became painfully apparent to the astonished and indignant Lennard Blair. With a darkening brow and a louring eye he approached the table, and the general expression of his face could not fail to arrest the attention of Mr. Cheatwood when he looked up, and, while shuffling the cards, asked if *he* had " any objection to a little mild play."

" Decidedly I have ; I never gamble—don't like it," was the blunt response, " yet, now that I think, I shall have a little écarté with you."

What Lennard had observed during the play between Dabchick and Cheatwood was known only to himself; he had seen enough, however, to con-vince him that Master Travice—to use plain language —was sharping ! He was enraged that such trickery should be practised in his own house, and all his smothered dislike of Cheatwood glowed to fever heat.

" How much to the point?" asked Cheatwood.

" Guinea points," replied Lennard, emptying a large glass of cool claret at the sideboard.

" Agreed."

" You look flushed, Mr. Dabchick."

" The evening is warm," sighed the poor lawyer, who was perspiring with irrepressible vexation.

" Try a glass of claret," said Lennard ; " there is some magnificent old port there—vintage '47—a favourite old dry wine of my father's. Or will you smoke a cigar outside till Feverley comes, and then we shall have our rubber ? He can't be long absent now—he might have bled and blistered all the people in Blairavon—rogues included by this time."

" Shall we divide for the deal ?" asked Cheatwood, who was all eagerness to begin.

" Have you prepared the pack ?"

" Yes—would you like to see for yourself ?" he asked, while running his fingers through his goatee beard, with a fidgety air.

" No, sir—I don't suspect you ; and here I see are all the twos, threes, fives, and sixes."

To decide the deal, the cards were cut at the commencement of the game, and the lowest card fell to Cheatwood, who dealt, and, as usual—won.

The deal then fell to Lennard, who played and lost again. Several games were played by them, but after the third Lennard had no more luck. Still, he seemed in no way discomposed ; he whistled, and talked on indifferent subjects—the last Derby—

Hesbia's style of playing—the extreme beauty of the evening, which had now given place to night, and Steinie had lighted candles; and ever and anon Lennard—to the manifest annoyance of Cheatwood—would stoop to pat and caress his father's otter terrier, Don, which lay under the table.

" Let us double the stakes," said Cheatwood.

" With pleasure," replied Lennard, who rose to assist himself to another glass of claret at the sideboard; but, as he had early been taught that a card-player should have at least four eyes, he made such good use of the two given him by nature that he distinctly saw Cheatwood, who was dealing, give himself *eight* cards, and skilfully contrive to drop three of these, till he could, by letting fall his handkerchief, or some other ruse, return them to the pack.

There was a heavy score against Lennard now, a decided hole would soon be made in the £100 he had brought with him from Liverpool, or, rather, in what remained of that sum; but he reseated himself with an air of unconcern, just as Feverley and Dabchick, who had been smoking outside, entered the room. By this time he was forty pounds in debt to Cheatwood.

" Still deep in écarté, Blair, eh? "

" Yes; rather too deep."

" It's a game I don't like."

" Nor I, Doctor; but I am playing for a purpose."

Cheatwood knit his brows, and darted a keen glance at the speaker, who was whistling again.

"What are you about, sir? is the terrier annoying you?" asked Lennard, sternly, as Cheatwood secured one of his dropped cards.

"I let a card fall, the king of trumps, by Jove! That scores one trick; play on, please."

"You dropped a card, did you?"

"Yes—awkwardly."

"You have dropped half the pack, throughout the evening; there are a whole handful of cards below the table, now!"

"Impossible; d—nation, what do you mean?" he demanded.

"Look, gentlemen, Feverley and Dabchick, look here," cried Lennard, furiously, as he tore aside the tablecloth, and there certainly were several cards seen lying close to the feet of Travice Cheatwood, who grew pale, dangerously pale, but who still sought to brazen the matter out.

"Cards are there, certainly," he stammered; "but how the deuce they came there, I am completely at a loss to understand."

"How is one to say an unpleasant thing in pleasant language?" asked Lennard, grimly.

"Why?"

"Because I am about to accuse you——"

"Of what, sir; of what?"

"Cheating and card-sharping; is that plain?"

" I repeat that I know nothing about these cards ; on my honour, I do ! "

" Honour—a card-dropper, a rascally sharper, talks of his honour ! "

" When you have quite done blowing off the steam, Mr. Blair, perhaps I may talk to you," said Travice, rising as if to withdraw, a ghastly glare in his light green eyes ; " till then——"

" Do you take me for a child, or a fool ? " demanded Lennard, starting between him and the door. " At least ten times this evening I have seen you drop your cards, and now that I have exposed you——"

" What do you mean to do ? kick up a row, eh ? " asked Travice.

" I give you the choice of leaving the house by the door, or a window. Up with the sash, Dab-chick," said Lennard, giving full swing to his pent-up dislike, and heedless even of what Hesbia or Mr. Vere might think.

" I shall prefer the door," replied Cheatwood, calmly, but with a terrible expression in his cold and cunning eye.

" You are wise."

" I am one to three."

" I would not willingly assault a man in my own house, even though he had sought to disgrace it by his conduct : but there is one little piece of business to be transacted ere you go, Mr. Cheatwood."

" To the point, sir; what is it? "

" You have won twenty pounds from Mr. Dabchick, this evening; but while the discovery of your mis-conduct cancels that debt of honour, it renders it necessary that you return his I O U for £50 now n your possession. I give you three minutes by that clock to do so, and if, at the end of that time, it is not given up, by the Heaven that hears me, I shall break every bone in your skin, and toss you head foremost out of the window ! "

Lennard's aspect was stern, resolute, and he seemed everyway capable of putting his ugly threat in execution.

Cheatwood looked at him with a white gleam of malice and hate in his eyes; then an attempted smile of derision spread over his face, as he de-liberately opened his pocket-book, tossed the docu-ment to Dabchick (who nervously and instantly tore it to shreds), and with an ironical bow left the room, and quitted the house, whistling the last street tune, but leaving an indescribable chill on the hearts of the three, more especially on that of Lennard, whose sudden gust of anger soon evaporated.

CHAPTER XVIII.

CROWDY OF THAT ILK.

"I THINK that a quiet glass of grog will not be unacceptable after this unseemly shindy, and in such a hot night, too," said Lennard, ringing the bell for Steinie; "I never was engaged in such a thing before, and I would to Heaven that it had happened anywhere else than in my own house," he added, as he thought of the future, and they drew their chairs round the table, on which Steinie placed glasses, and the liqueur-frame.

"He'll be for calling you out," said Feverley, laughing.

"Bah! if he does, I shall not go. The days for such things are luckily past; and even in the days when they were not past, one wasn't obliged to go out with a swindler and card-sharper."

"He'll work you mischief somehow, if he can," lisped Dabchick, who looked far from easy in his mind, and apprehensive, he knew not of what.

"Mischief, likely enough," replied Lennard, as

he thought of Hesbia Vere, and how much power his tie of cousinship and residence at Blairavon gave him.

Mr. Dabchick felt greatly relieved from monetary embarrassment by the turn affairs had taken, in the restoration and destruction of his I O U, and the cancelling of the further debt of honour, and being grateful to Lennard, made many mental vows to eschew écarté for ever.

" By Jove! never was present at such a scene ! " said he, after a pause; " Doctor, what did the fellow look like, when Blair taxed him as a cheat ? "

" Like a patient seated in a dentist's chair, anything but pleasant," replied the Doctor, mixing a glass of grog. " Peter Pindar says that we should

> Mind what we read in godly books,
> And *not* take people by their looks.

But his features bear the double stamp of open insolence and secret dishonesty."

" And then the expression of his eyes as he gave up that wretched paper of mine ! "

" Yes ; a graveyard in a winter day, is a jolly sight when compared thereto ; but his eyes were full of dangerous hate."

" Hate ? I hope to be able to defy him in anyway," said Blair, who had been sitting in silence and full of disagreeable thoughts. " If his uncle knew of to-night's work, he could, of course, no longer tolerate his presence at Blairavon. It would injure Mr. Vere in the estimation of his friend the baronet, with whom he has evidently every desire to stand well."

A strange expression, a very peculiar kind of smile that stole over the weak features of Dabchick and twinkled in his sore-looking eyes, made Lennard say,—

"Talking of Sir Cullender, by the way, I do not find his name, arms, or family recorded in any of the 'Baronetages' of Nova Scotia or Great Britain, and I have looked ever so far back."

"Pooh, my dear fellow!" said the little advocate, whose tongue was loosened by the good wine he had drunk, and whose heart was full of gratitude for the recent release from his double obligation to a cardsharper; "the whole affair is a dodge, a sham—a humbug!"

"What—the title?"

"Yes—the assumption of it, at least."

"How—I cannot comprehend this?"

"The fact is, that the man himself is, as you may see, a London Jew; his blood as old as Abraham's perhaps, but not a drop of it Scotch for all that."

"Do, please, explain all this enigma," urged Feverley, for Lennard was completely mystified.

"My friend little Mark Shoddy, the sheriff of a Scotch county, told me all about it," continued the dapper advocate, imbibing his grog with great relish;

" the baronet is one of the most singular dodgers I
ever met. He was once threadbare enough in London—thankful for something less even than a five
pound note; but he invented, or pretended to in-
vent—it is all the same at times—some useless
necessity, which he had patented; so a company was
formed under that remarkable system so favourable
to schemers, the Limited Liability Act. A board
was appointed with a fussy secretary and a fat and
respectable looking president. There was an office
with a board-room and secretary's-room, carpeted
with brown cocoa-nut matting, and hung with highly
glazed maps, mysterious diagrams, and gaudy pro-
spectuses; there were chairs upholstered in crimson
leather, flywire window blinds with gilded letters,
high desks and ditto chairs, and big ledgers and day-
books with flaming rededges. So he whose linen
had long been represented by a paper collar and a
dickey at most—both turned at times—who had
haunted low taverns at the East-end of London and
dined on a greasy chop with a pot of beer, or on a
biscuit with a refreshing draught of pump-water—
he, Benjamin Cullender Crowdy—soon came forth
in a new guise—a phœnix arisen from its ashes—a
caterpillar expanded to a butterfly, with a house at
the West-end and a villa at Richmond, with vineries
and pits for ice and forcing; a deer forest in the
Highlands, and a snipe bog in Ireland, though
he neither stalked in one nor shot in the other;

cellars with something better in the binns than cobwebs and dust; a box at the opera and a well-hung
carriage; but then, my dear sirs, you are aware that
we live in an age of progress, and it is a great country
this!"

"This?" queried the Doctor, "which do you mean
—Scotland or England?"

"I mean both, for knaves and hypocrites flourish
in both, with a success quite bewildering."

"But *what* is his particular business?" asked
Lennard.

"That is just what no fellow can understand,"
replied Dabchick; "but we all know that he is
Chairman of the Great Anglo-Saxon Beef and Mut-
ton Company; President of the Imperial, Life, Loan,
and Lucifer-match Office, and Extraordinary Director
of the Royal Joint-Stock Company for something
else, and that he is connected with heaven knows
how many more 'limited' affairs."

"If such is your view of this person, why do you
continue to reside with him at Blairavon?" asked
Lennard somewhat gravely, for these revelations
shocked and disgusted him.

"Mr. Vere is about to have a dispute concerning
a right of way to his coal pits at the Kaims, and my
legal advice is necessary; I expect to be retained in
the case by Soaper and Sawmsinger, W.S., his Edinburgh agents," replied poor Dabchick, colouring, for
he was of the many unbriefed, as we have said.

"But how about the baronetcy?" persisted Lennard, who thought that he was forgetting, or wandering from that part of the subject.

"That is the greatest dodge—the most clever stroke of all!" replied Dabchick, laughing.

"I cannot understand—he succeeded of course?" asked Lennard.

"I shall explain to you all about it; but first tell me if there is any dormant or defunct Blair baronetcy?"

"I don't know."

"The more is the pity."

"What matter—and why?"

"Because you might become Sir Lennard Blair to-morrow after the fashion of Crowdy of that Ilk. My friend Sheriff Shoddy—a great authority on family history and cavalier biographies is little Mark—about a year ago had a petition presented to him by a merchant of London, designating himself Sir Cullender Crowdy of that Ilk, for general service to Sir Ronald Crowdy of Crowdymoudy, Knight Baronet, who died in 1650, for the purpose of taking up the title. Shoddy, like a sharp lawyer, ordered proof of propinquity to be given; these proofs, of course, were never forthcoming; but Sir Cullender at once assumed the title, and had it duly engraved on his cards and on most gorgeous brass at his place of business in the city. Clever stroke that, was it not?"

" Mr. Vere should be told of all this," said Lennard, full of astonishment and indignation at the imposture.

" It is not my part, or my interest either, to injure a favourite guest in his estimation, especially as the man's wealth seems undoubted."

" Well, then, Hesbia—Miss Vere, I mean —"

" Oh, she, of course, cannot be supposed to understand the dodge of the title—perhaps doesn't wish to do so," was the significant and half-spiteful addition.

" You have tried to enlighten her, perhaps ? "

" Not exactly," replied the lawyer, carelessly ; but reddening under the searching eyes of Lennard ; " thus, as I have told you, Crowdy is a London Jew to the backbone. Of course, the Crowdys of what's-its-name were an old Lowland family."

" How came he to know about them ? "

" Probably when searching for a crest—every snob must have his bit of heraldry on his pasteboard now, and many a crest is there that never shone on a helmet in the line of battle—he had seen that the baronetcy is stated to have been *extinct* since 1650, when the last of the Crowdys was killed by the English at the battle of Inverkeithing ; but its extinction exactly suited Sir Cullender."

" This ought to be exposed," said Lennard, with growing anger ; " it is an impudent humbug—an infamous assumption."

"I think it a great joke. The line has been defunct for two centuries; but whose personal interest is it to expose the bosh, the sham of the thing, or to insist that, after two hundred years of obscurity as hewers of wood and drawers of water, the affinity, even if it actually existed, should be proved?"

"The Garter-king should interfere."

"He has no power whatever in Scotland, and our Lord Lyon is abolished, so people may play what pranks they please in the matter of arms and heraldry."

All this was a new view of the law of succession which rather bewildered Feverley and his host; but, as the night was far advanced now, they separated. Dr. Feverley rode off to the village, and Mr. Dabchick returned to Blairavon, escorted a portion of the way—as he felt nervous among the woodlands— by Lennard, who extracted from him a promise that he would not mention what had transpired lest it might pain and mortify Miss Vere.

The dapper lawyer promised this all the more readily as he was to leave Blairavon on the morrow for Edinburgh, giving Lennard—whom he was quite aware would return to Liverpool in three days—a pressing invitation to "look him up soon," adding, as the address of his "rooms," a good style of street, but omitting to add how many more of the faculty chummed with him in the same house, for the sake of economy and appearances, seeing the gaieties of life, through the medium of the "free list," and being the "utility men" of a penny daily—for in too many iustances to such small fry as these has the once brilliant bar of Scotland sunk.

CHAPTER XIX.

COME TO ME.

NEXT morning when seated alone in the breakfast parlour, Lennard lingered over his morning meal, and left his newspaper untouched and uncut. The freshest of eggs, the thickest of cream, pickled salmon grilse, and cakes of barley-meal—Elsie's own baking—with heather honey and so forth, remained nearly untasted and forgotten by Lennard.

Last night's row and its contingent revelations were uppermost in his thoughts, and the whole affair in all its details and suggestive suspicions proved a source of much distress and disgust to him. Though always distrustful of Travice Cheatwood, he had never thought him a positive swindler, yet the gambling of last night had proved him to be so; and of what other treachery was not such a man capable?

When the figure of Travice came before his mind's eye, notwithstanding his insolent brusquerie, his general accuracy of toilet, his careful evening suit of

black with silk facings, cuffs and studs, and prim-
rose-coloured gloves—his perfection of a tie, a
bouquet at his button-hole, his laced shirt and well-
waxed moustache—more than all, when he thought
of him as the cousin of Hesbia, he would ask of himself—"Have I been rash and harsh—*can* I have
mistaken him?" And then the stern conviction
that he had done right, and right only, came fully
and forcibly upon him.

Lennard could not, while he was at Blairavon,
and after all that had occurred, visit the Vere's,
even before departing for Liverpool.

That Mr. Vere should encourage attentions by a
character so doubtful as Mr. Dabchick represented
"the baronet" to be, caused to the young lover
the keenest mortification; it roused a spirit of
honourable and honest resentment, and gave him a
serious and most unpleasant doubt of Vere himself
—Vere, the man he had hitherto looked upon as the
mirror of integrity. With all this, he felt pity, too,
for Hesbia.

He would see Dabchick once more. Starting, he
looked at his watch, and found that by that time
the little lawyer was being bowled homeward along
the Edinburgh and Glasgow Line, or at that moment
was probably cooling his heels, and calculating the
limits of human patience, at the Carstairs Junction,
amid its Serbonian bog, if he went by the other
route; and Lennard smiled to himself, as he thought

of poor Dabchick's pressing but hazy offers of uncertain hospitality.

Ere leaving Oakwoodlee, he felt the necessity of seeing Hesbia at least once more, and alone, to end his own doubts, and to warn her of the baronet's unsound character, even at the risk of apparent jealousy. But he resolved not to mention the doings of Travice Cheatwood, lest he might thereby wound her feelings, for she had pride enough to be sensitive on a point of family honour.

"Oh, Hesbia!" thought he, "had you a brother to be your father's heir, or were you the heiress of something less than his enormous fortune, I might love you openly, and propose to you fearlessly; but as it is—alas! alas! poor devil that I am!"

Music, flowers, fans, and books, her silky silver-haired Skye terrier, little Fussy, he had given her, and even presents of more value, such as the pearl bracelet, and such as few girls would have accepted from a mere dangler; but all these she had taken with a brilliant smile and the prettiest words of thanks—taken as a matter of course; though he meant each and all for much more than that—each and all, the titles of songs and music, the subjects of selected books, and so forth, to have an import and significance that Hesbia, coquette as she was, could not fail to understand.

He hurried over his breakfast, and was about to open his desk for the purpose of writing to her, when old Stephen Hislop entered the room in a state of high excitement, his wrinkled cheeks and almost toothless jaws quivering with anger.

" Did you hear a shot near the house this morning, Mr. Lennard ? " he asked, holding up his hands, which were stained with blood.

" Some boys firing at the wood-pigeons, probably —but near the house, you say.   A shot—when ? "

" Within these ten minutes, I should think."

" No ; but why do you ask—has anything happened ? "

" Poor old Don has been shot ! "

" Where ? " asked Lennard starting up.

" Close by the yett in the hedge—the yett near the highway ; I found the puir animal bleeding on the gravel wi' a bullet in its body, just through the loins, and have carried it here."

As Don had been an old, faithful, and favourite retainer of his father—a present from Ranald Cheyne too—Lennard fully shared the indignation and concern of Steinie, whom he followed to the entrance-hall, where Elsie was pouring forth her commiseration over the dog, which had just died, for the blood was still oozing from the wound in its loins.

" Most singular it is that we heard no report. Are you certain that the poor dog was shot so near the house ? "

" Quite certain, Master Lennard," replied Steinie, who, from old habit, still viewed the head of the

Blairs as a boy or a youth. " There was a little
pool of blood where I found it, but not a drop
elsewhere.   Don lay where the shot had stricken
him down, for I heard his sudden cry of pain, and
went to the spot instanter, and there he was, wallow-
ing in his death agony, and biting the gravel, puir
beastie ! "

" And no one was near with a gun ? "

" Gun or not, there was no report—the dog fell
as if elf-shot ! "

" A most extraordinary circumstance ! "

" Exactly what Mr. Cheatwood said," added
Steinie.

" Was *he* there ? "

" He was passing along the road at the moment I
heard poor Don's terrible cry."

" And had he not a gun or other firearm ? " asked
Lennard, with darkening face.

" Nothing in his hand but a thick walking-
staff."

" Go to the police station, and offer a reward for
the discovery of the offender, and get, if you can,
the bullet with which the poor dog was killed."

Lennard was seriously concerned for this sudden
death of an old household pet, and felt extreme
exasperation against the unknown perpetrator of an
outrage so wanton. The bullet was brought to him
by Steinie; it was conical, with a little wooden
plug for expansion, and in size was something smaller

than those used for the ordinary Enfield rifles. It retained no odour of powder, or appearance of having been *fired;* but the blood amid which it had been imbedded might have washed those signs away.

Lest it might be required in evidence, Lennard put it carefully by in his desk, while Steinie buried the terrier under a moss-grown stone seat in the garden, where, for many a year in the soft summer evenings, and in those of the ruddy autumn, he had nestled beside the feet of his departed master; and old Hislop sighed and shook his white locks, muttering 'the while to himself, as those well on in years will do, as he hung on a nail in the parlour, among similar relics (such as bits, spurs, and the shoes of favourite hunters, that had long since passed from the sand-cart to the knacker's-yard), the little chain collar of the "auld master's otter terrier."

Of the somewhat trivial affair of the dog's death the great lumbering rural police could make nothing; so Lennard's reward was proffered at the turnpikes in vain; but there came a time when it was regarded as an important evidence in another matter.

Though greatly ruffled by this incident, with which he somehow mingled the idea of Travice Cheatwood, the thoughts of Lennard soon reverted to their former channel, and having but two days now to spare, he reopened his desk and pondered, pen in hand, on the fashion in which he was to address Miss Vere.

He had grown painfully sensible that, though still made welcome at the house of her father—though still free as of old to make presents of tickets, flowers, bouquets, and graceful trifles to Hesbia, and frequently to be her escort—that, as the baronet (whom he had never met before) became more intimate, she had grown more sisterly—at times even more distant in her bearing towards him.

To Lennard this was intolerable, after all the early years of pleasant intercourse and the terms on which they were.

If, from among her friends, Hesbia had been compelled to make choice of a husband, then Lennard Blair, by his handsome face and figure, his winning manners, and general air of distinction—their past companionship, and so forth, would undoubtedly have had the preference; but, then, he was poor, and she—in some respects—was not much better, being completely dependent on the will of her father.

Wealth and luxury, with all their pleasant concomitants, were as necessary to Hesbia's existence as air or sunshine. Her father's wealth was—she knew, and often had he told her so—liable to the sudden crashes, failures, and contingencies of trade;

so she paused ere she let her heart go *quite* out of her own keeping.

On the other hand, Lennard reflected : why should not he as well as any other man marry Hesbia, and so realize the golden dream of his poor father's deathbed—the restoration of the Blairavon lands and manor-house to the old line of Blair. Better it seemed that he should become its proprietor— bred as he was to trade, cautious, and steady—than a person like Sir Cullender, or it might be some penniless and spendthrift peer.

Business training had made Lennard Blair careful and thrifty; the experience gained at the desk in Liverpool would be eminently useful at home. Then with the brilliant Hesbia for his wife, how happily would time glide away at Blairavon. All the future would be but an anticipated part of Paradise.

Intimate though he was with Hesbia Vere, on *this* occasion Lennard wasted a dozen sheets of note-paper ere he schemed out a few lines to the effect that, owing to an unpleasant affair which had taken place at his house last night, he was unable to visit Blairavon while Mr. Travice Cheatwood resided there ; and, as he had to start for Liverpool in two days, he begged that she would grant him an inter-view, that he might take leave of her alone, as he had much to explain. "*Come to me* at any hour or place you may name, for there I shall be waiting," he wrote, and concluded by imploring her to do so, as, on reaching Liverpool, he would probably have to go at once and for an indefinite period to South America.

"If I possess any real interest in her eyes or in her heart, this must surely rouse it," thought he.

"My dear Miss Vere," he added, in a postscript, "you may write me a note *so worded*, that even if it falls into the hands of another, its true meaning will not be understood."

Lennard had an eye to Cheatwood when he wrote thus; but when he had sealed up the note, he found that his *fidus Achates*, Steinie, had gone out in search of a salmon grilse, for the good old fellow was never idle. So Lennard went forth himself in search of a fitting messenger to take his missive to the great house—one upon whom he could depend for placing it safely in Hesbia's hands.

He had not proceeded far along the highway bordering the closely-mown and smoothly-rolled lawn of Blairavon, when the sound of merry voices led him to look through the closely clipped beech hedge, and there he could see Cheatwood with Hesbia and the two Miss Cheynes, mallet in hand, and all intent on croquet—the girls becomingly dressed in summer hats and white piqués.

"Heavens!" thought he; "if old Ranald Cheyne knew the real character of the fellow his girls are playing with!"

And now, as chance would have it, he overtook Mademoiselle Savonette, Hesbia's French maid, with whom he had the good fortune to be an especial favourite. She was a handsome, dark girl, with a bright and pleasing expression, rather lady-like in her dress and bearing, but with strongly-defined eyebrows, and a slight indication of a moustache darkening her upper lip, particularly in the corners of her curved and very pretty mouth.

"Good morning, m'sieu," said she, with her thick, French burr, bowing and smiling; "are you going to join miladi and the demoiselles at croquet?"

"No, mademoiselle," he replied, "I am unfortunately pressed for time, and leave this to-morrow for England."

"So soon!—and we have seen so leetle, oh so ver' leetle of you at the château yonder!"

"Ah, you will see still less, I fear, my good friend Savonette; but will you do me a favour?"

"A thousand if I can—m'sieu is always so ver' polite to me."

"Give this note to Miss Vere on the earliest opportunity, and bring me the reply, if you can do so with convenience; if not, post or send it."

"I shall have ze greatest gratification, m'sieu," replied Savonette, almost blushing with pleasure at what seemed to savour of a good share in an intrigue. "Tres bon! tres bon!" she added, as she pocketed the note together with the sovereign

which Lennard adroitly left in her hand as he kissed
and pressed it; and then, lifting his hat to the
pretty soubrette, walked back to Oakwoodlee, very
well pleased with the first stage of matters.

How little could he foresee all that was to follow,
and that, instead of departing for Liverpool, the
morrow would find him still at Oakwoodlee!

CHAPTER XX.

TRAVICE RE-OPENS THE TRENCHES.

THE event of the preceding evening and other discoveries that were certain to be made in the fulness of time, rendered Travice Cheatwood as thoughtful and dull over his croquet as Lennard Blair had been over his breakfast. Even Hesbia's high-arched instep displayed from time to time upon a ball, exhibiting the dainty kid boot, the smooth white stocking, over a lovely and tapering ankle, could not lure him to forget the devil that occupied his heart.

The minds of both gentlemen were occupied by the same object, though they regarded her from two very different points of view. Travice was desperately resolved to make one more effort to secure her love—or that which he valued much more, her hand—as a protection to himself amid discoveries that were inevitable, and to insure a right over whatever she might possess.

His more immediate troubles were likely to arise

from a " kite "—one of those " little bills " which he
was incessantly having " done," and very often to the
undoing of others; and his failure in rooking Lennard and the other two would prevent him meeting
this when it fell due—a circumstance which inflamed
his fury against his detector.

The croquet, a game which he loathed from its
extreme slowness, and luncheon, too—perhaps the
most pleasant meal in a country-house—were both
over.   Mr. Vere was writing to Mr. Envoyse, in the
library, for he possessed one, though he never read
anything beyond " Bradshaw," the *Times'* money
article, or the *Mark Lane Express.*   The baronet
was inditing one or two telegrams for London ; the
Cheyne girls were in the drawing-room, trying over
the excruciating Tannhauser overture; and, to the
extreme astonishment and satisfaction of Travice,
he was invited by Hesbia to accompany her on an
exploring expedition through a portion of the house
in which she had never been before, so the colour
mounted to his usually pale cheek, and his heart—
or that which passed for such—beat quicker and
more lightly.

" Everything in this world is a fluke," said he,
" so here goes ! "

The part of the manor-house through which they
proceeded was one that had remained almost untouched in its architecture or furniture during at
least three generations of the Blairavon family, and

it seemed, in fact, to be a series of lumber-closets or queer corridors, and little wainscoted chambers, with one or two turret stairs, and steps up, and steps down, where shins might be broken and skirts torn; little windows were there, thickly grated with iron and half darkened by interwoven cobwebs and depending ivy or the upper branches of the old trees without, giving a dubious light to these places, while there was about them a dusty, damp, and mouldy odour, which seemed to be emitted by the old lumber lying forgotten there, such as square-backed chairs of the Covenanting times, covered with tapestry or faded Utrecht velvet; tripod tables or gueridons of buhl and ebony of the days of James VII.; Chinese screens and japan cabinets of the First and Second Georges,—and Hesbia wandered among this chaos as if she had penetrated into a hitherto unknown and uninhabited land. The girl had taste enough to be delighted.

"Oh! Travice," she exclaimed, her brown eyes sparkling with pleasure, "when next we act charades, won't these things come splendidly in for scenery?"

"Some of old Blairavon's Wardour Street antiquities, I suppose," grumbled Travice; yet among these faded relics were some of the household *lares* of old Richard Blair; "a beastly old hole," continued Travice; "but we are alone in it any way. Save for you, Hesbia, I would soon cut this deadly lively den and be off by the first express train for the south."

"But for me?" she exclaimed, as she seated herself in one of the old tapestry chairs, from which the moths flew out as she did so; "surely I do nothing to hamper your movements or to alter your plans, whatever they may be."

"You alike order and derange the whole progress of my life, Hesbia."

"Travice, don't deal in paradoxes."

"May I repeat again, how dearly I love you?" he said in an earnest whisper.

"Pray don't, Travice; it becomes stale, flat, and unprofitable from unimpassioned repetition."

"Indeed!" said he through his clenched teeth.

"There is plenty of love on your tongue, but not a trace of it in your eyes; so pray do not attempt to act the part," she replied, laughing. "With my hair powdered over a toupee and a Pompadour dress, wouldn't I make a picture in this old chair, with my dimpled elbow on that buhl table and the Japan cabinet behind? Then you might come in as my adorer—a Sir Charles Grandison or a Scottish cavalier—at my feet."

"Hesbia," he continued, keeping down his wrath, coming as close to her as he dared, and leaning over her as he lowered his voice, "I shall get a special license by return of post, and ——"

"What are you talking about, Travice?" said

she, with one of her merriest and most musical
bursts of laughter. "You forget that, even if you
had a bride, which you have *not*, so far as I am
concerned, a license from the Archbishop of Canter-
bury would be as useless here as a cheque on the
Bank of Elegance."

"Why?"

"Because we are in Scotland."

Though desperation and monetary difficulties imparted something of real depth and earnestness to
all he said, finding that he made no progress, and
that she still bantered him, he became, perhaps
naturally, irritated, and the native insolence of his
character caused him to adopt a brusquerie of bearing but ill-suited to the submissive part of a real
lover.

"Tell me, my wicked cousin, is my rival the
baronet or Mr. Blair?"

"You have rivals in both, perhaps," replied
Hesbia, with her bright hazel eyes half closed,
while she clasped and unclasped Lennard's bracelet
on a wrist that was white as the pearls themselves.

"Now that the absurd old boy who sold this place
is gone, what will his son Lennard have in possession
—a dozen of silver spoons, a baptismal mug (oh, the
people of this sour Presbyterian country don't believe in such holiday vanities as god-parents), well, a
family Bible, the old boy's dram-bottle, of course,
and his last blessing in broad Scotch."

"Travice," said Hesbia, her soft face clouding with real annoyance, "how cruel of you to talk thus, and how bad is the taste that inspires you to do so!"

"Come, Hesbia, be sensible," he resumed, bending over her again; "you can't care for this fellow. I hate your 'has beens'—your shabby-genteel people! There is no one so amusingly vain or so profound a bore as a reduced gentleman—a Scotch or Irish one particularly."

Hesbia's full, red lip curled and quivered slightly, but she made no reply, so Travice continued in his own peculiar style.

"I suppose this fellow thinks himself a trump-card here, since he has returned to his own place like the travelled monkey who has seen the world," sneered Travice.

"He has come back, poor fellow, to all that remains of what was once his place."

"Jolly jealous and envious he must be of your governor, who owns nearly the whole of it."

"You judge of his heart by your own, Travice."

"Is it proper or becoming that you should be always flirting and philandering with this fellow, as I have heard you did in Liverpool?"

"How, sir?" asked Hesbia, growing absolutely pale with anger.

"With a mere clerk in your father's counting-room," continued Travice, with irrepressible wrath, as he found himself blundering on the verge of a quarrel.

"A partner in the firm, you mean, Travice."

"Idiots, to take one of his country in at all. However humble or mean the snob may be in a firm, he always creeps up to be chief of it some day. I forget what Macauley says in his history about this sort of thing."

"How long would you be in rising so?" taunted Hesbia.

"Besides, a partner—ha, ha! I doubt very much if his name will ever appear as such in the books, if they are aired some fine day in the Bankruptcy Court," said Travice, with one of his ugliest smiles, which Hesbia totally failed to understand. "I am but ill inclined to render you without a struggle to such a lover, Hesbia," he continued, attempting to take her hand between his; "for I thank Fate that I know a little of life, and am not like him."

"In what way?"

"A kind of ass, who quotes Byron and Bunyan, and spends his evening in holding wools for girls to wind and unwind."

"Byron and Bunyan—such a conjunction—Don Juan and the Pilgrim's Progress!" exclaimed Hesbia, with a genuine burst of laughter, which increased the growing rage of Cheatwood; but he, too, gave a kind of laugh, and, laying a hand upon her soft and half-averted shoulder,—

I.   Q

"Listen to me, dear Hesbia," said he; "I am not a bad kind of fellow in general; I would agree with the devil himself——"

"If you saw that it was your interest to do so. You must not forget, cousin, that we have known each other since childhood."

"And your experience teaches you that I shall probably come to an evil end, like the bad boy in the spelling-book."

"I hope not, Travice, for the sake of the blood we share in common, and for your father's memory."

"By Jove! I know nothing about him, except what a handsome marble slab in the church of St. Martin-in-the-Fields, at Liverpool, tells me—that he seems to have commenced life, like your father, as a boy at the Bluecoat School, and must have been jolly rich, to judge by the many virtues ascribed to him in gilt letters, though he left me poor enough, God knows!"

"He was a man who stood well with the world, Travice."

"The world? Curse the world! I shake my clenched hand in its hypocritical face—snap my fingers at it, and spurn alike its pity and its patronage!" exclaimed Travice, while a terribly malignant expression shone in his pale green eyes. "What is it, Hesbia, that one gets for nothing in this world?"

"Why, nothing, I suppose."

"Exactly."

"It is a detestable idea, though."

"It is truth, as my experience of it has been."

There was a moment of silence; and Travice, as he looked at Hesbia, seated in the antique chair among all the quaint lumber, in a brilliant blue silk trimmed with white lace, seemed, even to his un-artistic eye, a lovely picture. In the sunlight that shone through the deeply embayed and ancient window behind, her hair, which was a rich brown in the shade, seemed then a golden red; her face was half in shadow; her dark-brown pencilled brows lent a piquancy to the soft eyes which formed her greatest fascination, but there was a provoking smile on the beautiful lips, which some might have thought too large and full. The fine texture of her colourless skin, the symmetry of her hands and arms all made up a charming whole, though her figure seemed moulded on a scale that promised perhaps over-stoutness in the years to come. Travice thought, that after a period of matrimony, one might tolerate the change.

"Listen to me, Hesbia, for it is the last time I shall ever address you, on this subject at least," said Travice, with a tone of passion for the first time in his voice; "but you must promise not to laugh at me."

"I promise. Say on Travice."

He drew nearer, but whatever he was about to say, a malediction came instead; for threading her

way among the lumber of the closet appeared
Mademoiselle Savonette, whose dark eyes were
sparkling with malevolent pleasure, as she had an
especial dislike for Travice Cheatwood, who was
always grasping and kissing her on sly occasions,
yet never gave her even a crownpiece to buy a
ribbon or pair of gloves. She saw at once that she
had come at a time most inopportune for him, and
she now resolved to give him a further sting if
possible.

"A letter for miladi. Pardonnez moi, M'sieu
Sheetwood," said the black-browed Abigail with a
low curtsy.

"A letter, Hesbia. Thank Heaven it is not for
me," said Cheatwood, affecting to laugh. "Nothing
ever finds me out but old bills, and they or their
senders are inexorable. Fair cousin, you look dis-
turbed—as the novels say. What's up?"

"It is from M'sieu Blair," continued Savonette.

Hesbia reddened with evident confusion and
annoyance, but tore open the note, saying as her
smiling maid withdrew,—

"What on earth does he write to me about. I
don't think I have any of his books or secrets
either?"

"Is your note actually from that fellow Blair?"

"Yes; how strange!" said Hesbia, with such a
pretty air of wonder that one might have thought
Lennard had never written to her before.

" What does he want, or mean?" asked Cheatwood, with a deepening frown on his face. " Is the fellow mad that he writes to you?"

" He simply mentions that an unfortunate circumstance will prevent him from visiting Blairavon prior to his departure. What can it be?"

" How should I know?" was the sullen response.

" You quarrelled last night, that seems evident."

" He certainly caught that legal adventurer, little Dabchick, cheating me at écarté; there was a bit of a row, and that was all," replied the unabashed Travice.

" Impossible!—Mr. Dabchick cheat at cards! The poor little creature has not the brain of a snipe; he never could win a game from me, even when we played for bonbons or a pair of gloves. Tell me instantly all about it," she added, colouring with real vexation; " how did it happen?"

" Well, you know——" Travice began slowly.

" No I don't know!" she interrupted him impetuously.

" Well, you see——" he faltered.

" I don't see—I *hear*," exclaimed Miss Vere, beating the floor with her foot as she started from her chair.

" Bother! how is a fellow ever to get on with such a spitfire as you?"

" Any way you have had a low quarrel at cards."

"One must always have cash in hand, Hesbia. What the blind goddess omits to give us, blind hookey or écarté sometimes will."

"Travice, Travice; I say it with sorrow, you have long since lost your reputation for honour."

"Have I? Well, Hesbia, I have never missed it, and, for some years, have been jolly enough without it."

"Take care, sir; you have a notoriety——"

"An attribute apt to become annoying and expensive," replied her unabashed cousin.

"But to pluck people at cards——"

"You wrong me, Hesbia. People do not win at cards always by legerdemain, but by exercising the brains that God has given them. It is simply science against folly, mind against matter. It is memory and observation."

"Knowing the backs as well as the fronts of the cards—eh?"

"No; but having a lightning eye, a quick hand, a memory of sequences, a memory that never fails— these enable me to win at cards; but, enough of this! I would speak of my passion, my love for you, Hesbia——"

"Enough of *that*, say I, and let us recur to it no more," said she emphatically, as she swept away from his presence with an expression of resolution and coldness in her great brown eyes, such as he had never seen there before, and which there could

be no mistaking. The pretty smile, that from childhood she had been in the habit of according to all,
whether they pleased her or not, had quite passed
out of her face.

Cheatwood stood for a time with a dark expression
in his pale eyes, and a cruel one on his thin lips,
as he gnawed his moustache and ran his fingers
viciously through his goatee-beard.

"She has gone to answer that beast's note," he
muttered ; "and that answer I must and shall see,
as the best means of discovering the actual terms on
which they stand with each other."

And though a coward in soul, a craven at heart,
Travice Cheatwood felt towards Lennard Blair all
the hateful spirit of another Cain glow within him !

CHAPTER XXI.

THE SECRET LETTER.

AWARE that it must be by fraud or cunning, and not by force, that he could obtain a sight of any answer which his cousin might send to Lennard Blair, Travice, after observing that she was seated at her desk, and at a little buhl table in the inner drawing-room, writing — an occupation the sight of which filled him with the keenest jealous suspicions—Travice, we say, after remarking this, stole out to the avenue, there to watch the departure of any servant or other messenger towards Oak-woodlee; but without a thought as to how he was to intercept the missive, for neither the intellect or imagination of Travice were of the highest order.

He hovered near the gate-lodge, and after a delay of about twenty minutes, saw the page—the "Buttons" of the household—coming down the avenue with a note in his hand. The heart of

Cheatwood beat fast with mingled pain and impatience!

Ideas of open bribery or of violence immediately occurred to him, only to be dismissed, as either would lead to ultimate detection and a final quarrel. What was to be done—to what device could he resort to secure even a sight of the note, and let it go to its destination after?

Boylike, the little messenger made several détours, dances, and gyrations from the gravelled carriageway, round the bay-trees, cypresses, and clumps of shrubbery that grew among the smoothly mown grass of the lawn; and during one of these performances, while he was indulging himself in a species of break-down dance and singing a few lines of the last street-song, Cheatwood contrived to throw a walking-stick between his legs in such a skilful manner as to trip him up, and poor Buttons fell heavily on his hands and face amid the rough gravel of the avenue.

His hat, with its lace band and cockade (it had one to please the vanity of Hesbia), rolled off in one direction, while the wind blew the note from his hand in another.

Ere he had gathered himself up and looked about, Cheatwood's foot was planted adroitly on the billet, and the boy, with a lugubrious expression, looked around for it in vain. The page was young enough to be on the point of tears; he had scratched and torn his hands, soiled his livery, and lost the note—a triple calamity!

"Now, Mr. Cheatwood," said he, "after having your joke and knocking me over as if I was skittles or Aunt Sally, perhaps you'll help me to find my young lady's note, or I'm blow'd if there won't be a jolly row about it."

"Look alive, Buttons, and you'll be sure to see it somewhere."

"Not while you're a-standing on it, sir," replied the boy, whose sharp eye saw that a portion of the note was visible from under the heel of Cheatwood's boot.

"The devil! and so I am," said he, stooping and picking it up with a glow of rage, that deepened when he saw that it was addressed to Blair, and in Hesbia's handwriting.

"Now, sir, the note, if you please," said the boy, boldly.

"It is for Mr. Blair at Oakwoodlee, I perceive."

"Yes, sir."

"Were you to wait for an answer?"

"No—just to deliver it, and come slick off; but look how precious dirty you have made it," added the boy, beginning to whine; "I can never, by no manner of means, give it to a gentleman in that state!"

"And you cannot take it back to your mistress," said Travice.

"It was all along o' you, sir!" exclaimed the boy, whose eyes were now full of tears.

"Did Miss Vere give it to you in person?"

"No, sir."

"Who, then?" asked Cheatwood, wishing to gain time for consideration.

"Mamselle Savonette; and she got it from the wally, who said as it was a hinvite to dinner. I ain't noways to blame, and I'll tell Mr. Blair and Miss Hesbia so, though she guv me warning that the next mistake as I committed, after treading on Fussy's tail, I should go back by the fust train for Liverpool."

"You shall do nothing of the kind. Here, Buttons, I have got you into a scrape, and I shall get you out of it, if I can," said Cheatwood, giving the boy a crown, an unparalleled piece of liberality on his part. "Run to the gate-lodge, and get from the keeper's wife a clean envelope, a pen and ink—quick as greased lightning—and I'll wait for you here."

Brushing his hat with his cuff to smooth the nap, as he ran, Buttons—a sharp, town-bred boy—started at full speed to the gate-lodge, while Cheatwood, without a moment of hesitation, tore open the envelope, and made himself master of the contents, which ran thus :—

"*I shall be* much obliged (as I have to make a sketch at the stile *on the path to Craigellon,* which will be one of *about nine* I am preparing for my album) if you could kindly let me have some crayons, of which I am quite out. *To-morrow evening* will suit. I *do not* know a more pleasant occupation than drawing, and trust it will not *fail* me for many a year *to come.* Believe me, yours ever,

"HESBIA VERE."

In the veiled language of such correspondence the flirt was perfect. There was a flattering subtlety in the letter having no real beginning—no intro-ductory phrase; thus the imagination of the reader was at full liberty to supply the most endearing epithets; and though she knew by past experience that Lennard Blair would be conscious that he was to read, as the real meaning of her letter, only the *underlined* words, she had not the slightest idea that they would be read, and equally well understood, by a third party.

The plan was, perhaps, a shallow one; but after being puzzled for a minute, and supposing that the word "crayons" alone concealed the mystery, Travice Cheatwood, as he ran his eye a second time over Hesbia's note, took in the hidden sense of it at once, and then saw that it was a regular assignation to meet at the stile on the path to Craigellon at nine

o'clock the following evening, with the tender addition, "do not fail to come."

If proofs of a secret understanding were required,
he held them in his hand beyond a doubt, and something like a hoarse and bitter malediction escaped
him ere he was aware that Buttons was by his side.
He now saw, or thought he saw, the reason why
Hesbia received his oddly and brusquely paid
addresses with a banter that bordered on contempt!

The "henwelloper," as Buttons called it, was not
quite so fine in its texture as that used by Hesbia,
which Travice tore into very small pieces, and put in
his pocket, being too cautious even to scatter the
white shreds on the green turf. He placed the note
in its new cover, addressing it in a hand as closely
resembling Hesbia's as he could achieve, and gave it
to the messenger.

"Now, Buttons, my sharp one," said he, "pocket
your crown and keep dark about this, or it may prove
a worse affair than treading on Fussy's tail!"

"All right, sir," said the liveried imp with a finger
on one side of his snub-nose and a look of intense
cunning in his large protruding grey eyes. He then
touched his hat and soon vanished on the path to
Oakwoodlee.

From habit and his own evil training, and through
the character of those among whom his lot in life
had been cast, or rather among whom he had cast
himself—for men are often the makers of their own

destiny—it was the nature of Travice Cheatwood to assign to every human creature the worst possible motives for every action in life.

Hence he saw in this proposed meeting at the stile on the path which led to Craigellon, a lonely and sequestered place in a rural district, but a portion of a deep intrigue; and while he ground his sharp teeth at the idea, he resolved that he would frustrate the interview at every hazard.

Should he be there in person? He had no precise right to interfere; but the simple fact of his presence might mar the object of their secret meeting. Should he bring Mr. Vere to the spot, or have Hesbia shut up? She was not a girl now, and was rather too womanly and too imperious by nature and temperament to endure constraint; and if the circumstance of *his* interference was in any way discovered by Hesbia, all hope of his success for the future would be over for ever!

He had not much time for considering what he should do, so Mr. Travice Cheatwood was between the horns of a dilemma, and turned into a cool and shady copsewood, where the broad-leaved fern and rank grass grew rich and deep in all their summer fragrance, to think over the matter undisturbed and in solitude.

"I am sick of flying kites—bills, those cursed acceptances, which at one time or other are sure to fall due—so inexorably due! Something must be done—but *what?* I shall not, if I can help it, let Hesbia shunt me on one side for a smooth-tongued snob like Blair, or for that shady baronet either, though she keeps both as strings to' her bow. If Hesbia won't have me, and Uncle Vere won't ' book-up' again, my look out is rather a bad one," he muttered gloomily. "Done on the Derby, done on the Oaks; exposed by that fellow Blair— d—n him; and *that bill, too!* Old Envoyse has already got wind of it. Oh, my God, where will all this end?"

He clenched his hands, ground his teeth, and wiped his forehead, down which some clammy drops were trickling.

" Shall I for ever be a Bohemian !" he exclaimed, with something like an imprecation and a groan mingled, " shall I for ever be doomed to trudge along the shady, and never on the sunny side of the road of life? Yet I have had my chances; every fellow has them at some time or other (so old Vere says, at least), and like a fool I have thrown them away. Perhaps so; but I may have one throw of the dice left yet—in Hesbia."

He remembered what he had heard Mr. Vere say, when suddenly he had come upon him and Sir Cullender, of his desire to possess Blair's little place, called Oakwoodlee, and his intention of then settling, by a trust deed during his life, and while solvent, the entire estate of Blairavon on Hesbia; and a black storm of fury seemed to gather in the heart of Travice, as he thought of all he might lose by Lennard's successful rivalry.

He was still lingering in the woods when the bell rang for dinner, and he found that evening had already drawn on, and that he had to hasten home to complete a hurried toilette.

All that evening during dinner and after it, while lingering in the drawing-room, Cheatwood was un-disguisedly silent and spiritless. Flora Cheyne, who was a lively and ladylike girl, did her best to rouse him, but strove in vain; for he was too sulky—too ill-bred in fact—to act a part he did not feel, while Hesbia, who was studying him closely, almost flattered herself that it was love for her and dis-appointment consequent to the sharp and final rejection of that morning.

That it was disappointment there could be little doubt; but, added thereto, were jealousy, avarice, and hate; the dread of a shameful detection, and the maturing of a desperate purpose.

He pleaded that he felt indisposed—had smoked too much, he feared—or perhaps it was the walnuts at dinner and so forth, when Mr. Vere remarked his strange appearance; and times there were when his aspect was so wretched that Hesbia, who was naturally kind and good-natured, tried to flatter, soothe, and cheer him; but this change of bearing on her part, served only to exasperate, as it failed to inspire him with the hope that through her means his embarrassments might pass away.

Without real love for her, his blasé heart was full of jealousy ; dread of the coming toils—toils that must inevitably close around him—with avarice and intense selfishness, filled up the measure of his misery. He imbibed much wine that night, more than ever Hesbia had seen him take since he came to Blairavon, and all the following day he required from the butler such a plentiful supply of brandy and soda, that the sleek and portly custodian of the wine-binns was quite perplexed ; and ever and anon Travice would mutter, while the glass rattled against his teeth, for his hands shook nervously,—

" Whatever I have to do to-night, the more I drink, the more fit I shall be to do it ! "

As this fatal evening drew on, he never lost sight of Hesbia. In his desperate soul his ideas as yet were vague, and the quantity he had imbibed over-night, and during the past day, had certainly not served to lessen that peculiar emotion of expansion which all wrongs or slights assume when viewed through the medium of alcohol.

The sun was in the west, and the evening was as beautiful and balmy as any lovers could desire it to be, when Hesbia, who had some intuitive dread of Travice, conceived a plan for getting him out of the way, and sending him in a direction exactly opposite to that of her trysting place.

I.   R

On the lawn before the house, he was lingering after dinner, amid the greenery of the grass, and the rustling of the trees, whose wavy shadows fell eastward far athwart it now; but to him the green cloth of the billiard-table was worth all the verdure of nature. His eyes were bloodshot; his cheeks rather paler than usual, and his fair moustache hid the dark and unhealthy hue of his lips. He was still in his dinner dress, and absently held a cigarette between the fingers of a daintly-gloved hand, and put it in his mouth from time to time, totally unconscious that it was quite unlit, or had long since gone out.

"Will you do me a great favour, Travice, dear?" asked Hesbia, who suddenly appeared before him, with a roll of music in her hands, and one of her wonderful and winning smiles in her clear hazel eyes.

"I'll do anything in the world for you, Hesbia," said he, in a voice that was husky.

"Last night Flora Cheyne forgot Tannhauser, and some other music, which I know she requires. Will you have the kindness to walk down to the Haughs with them for me—for her, I should say? It is only a mile beyond the mains of Kaims; the road is beautifully wooded."

"Ah—indeed."

"And you are such a favourite with dear Flora!"

"Pleasant—very."

Hesbia paused, for though she had got up her brightest and most pleading expression for the occasion, it was practised in vain; for Travice, not being naturally a lover, looked on the bright face, the seductive eyes, and wavy hair, with coldness, hardness, and distrust, while he thought,—

"How sweetly she can smile on 'dear Travice,' when she has a secret object to serve, some little game in view."

"The evening is beautiful," said he; "will you accompany me?"

"Impossible!" said Hesbia, colouring.

"Why?" he asked, with knitted brows.

"I have to write letters—to see the housekeeper, the cook, and attend to ever so many things; but if you decline to do me this little service, Travice, I can send a servant, or one of the under-gardeners," she replied.

"I do not decline; but I must make some change in my dress."

"Thanks, Travice, dear. I knew that I had but to ask, and you would be sure to oblige me," she replied, and, patting his hand, placed the roll of music in it, and, gathering her flowing skirt with singular grace, tripped through one of the low windows of the drawing-room, and disappeared, after giving him a brilliant smile, and a kiss blown from the tips of her fingers; while with a strange grimace on his features, and an ugly word on his tongue,

Travice, who shrewdly suspected *why* he was
sent in a direction exactly opposite to Craigellon,
ascended to his room to make some change in his
dress.

His mind was a chaos of bitterness and wrath.

The heat of the summer evening seemed stifling.
Who the deuce, he thought, could have expected
such an atmosphere in the North? His throat was
parched; he cast off coat, vest, and necktie. He
had already drained his water-carafe. He tried a
havannah, a cigarette, and a pipe in turn; but all
were failures to soothe.

Was he going mad, or should he get vulgarly
drunk in earnest? His hand was on the bell-rope,
and then he withdrew it, for he was nervously infirm
of purpose.

No; reason, reflection, fear, prevented him from
imbibing more than he had already done at dinner,
lest he should commit some extravagance, and be-
tray himself; for whatever outrage or trick he
might be tempted to perpetrate for the purpose of
preventing the interview at the stile, and its too
probable revelations from taking place, the instinct
of self-preservation remained intact and strong in
the mind of Mr. Travice Cheatwood.

" Well, well, in a month or so the game will be
up with me at last—played out," he muttered,
" and *this* affair more or less won't be much in
the sum total of delinquency. Anyway, I may

have to deprive this country of the benefit of my society, and go to America, the devil, or anywhere."

And he remembered that he had only about five sovereigns to carry him to any of the places so vaguely indicated.

He looked hastily round the room, which was too luxuriously furnished to be relinquished without regret. Shining above the tops of the old trees, the evening sun was streaming cheerily in, and a red spark seemed to fill the eyes of Travice, as they fell upon a weapon in a corner—his air-gun—the same by means of which he had shot the terrier, Don, the real or pretended caressing of which had led to the card-dropping discovery.

In an evil moment had Travice Cheatwood won that illegal weapon from a poaching companion at cards. Often had he been inclined to sell or throw it away, lest he might be tempted, as he was now, in a dark hour, to use it with a fatal effect; so often is it the case, that the power of doing mischief will cause mischief to be done.

He had already thought of its effect—silent, noiseless, deadly, and sure; and had striven to turn a deaf ear to the bad promptings of his evil angel; but now his eyes lit up with a strange malevolence as he looked at it.

He was certain that none in Blairavon knew that he possessed such a weapon; for, to the casual eye, it appeared to be only a large and heavy walking-staff.

"If it is to be done at all, why not be done now—now, when I am in the mood for it? But I must not kill him if I can help it; though hating him with the hatred of a devil," he muttered; "I must only seek to maim—only seek to maim—it may be to disfigure him for life, and then he'll fail to please the dainty eye of the flirting Hesbia Vere!"

He took up the pneumatic weapon, removed what seemed to be merely the knob of the stick, examined its barrels, lock, and trigger, and as he did so a grim, but desperate calm, seemed to come over him. Then to his eye the light appeared to darken, and the atmosphere to become more stifling; he rose to throw open the window, and felt the floor as if unsteady under his feet when he walked. It seemed to heave up and down, and to meet his steps half-way. Strange things, he thought, were passing round hishead a nd whispering in his ears.

"Bah!" said he, suddenly rallying, as he dropped a few bullets in the pocket of a shooting-jacket he had donned; "I must not allow the cursed super-stition called 'conscience' to mar my fortune in any way. One good shot to-night, and then this gun must leave my hand for ever!"

And he who yesterday only shrunk nervously from the exposure of a card-sharping row, was now—"so quickly do men's steps acquire an impetus on the downward path "—stealing forth without necktie or vest, armed, and almost heedless whether or not he committed an assassination.

He still carried, however, the roll of music, which he meant to deliver at the lodge of the Haughs, in time, he' hoped, to prevent the meeting at the stile on the path to Craigellon.

CHAPTER   XXII.

WILL THEY MEET?

THE sun was just dipping beyond the western hills, an undulating line of dark purple against the amber sky, and then Hesbia knew that it would be nearly a half-hour's walk in the twilight, ere she reached the place where she promised to grant the interview to Lennard Blair.   The last red rays were lingering on the tops of the trees, on the gilt vanes and carved gablets of the old manor-house— little pediments which bore the stag's head caboshed and the cognizance of many an alliance of the old line of Blairavon.

She did not issue forth by the avenue, as she knew that the baronet and her father generally had a quiet cigar there together about that time; but she went through the garden, where the deep old box-edging bordered the long ribbon-like stripes of verbenas, calceolarias, and geraniums, which now wore all their gayest hues; past the old and quaintly-

carved sun-and-moon dial, which bore the arms of
the Blairs, with the date 1590; past the vineries
and great conservatory, till she reached and opened
a little private gate that led to the spacious lawn
(which has not been ploughed, but ever under grass,
since the Union of the Crowns, according to the
Gazetteer of Scotland), and walked with hasty pace
to reach the roadway, that led almost directly to
the narrow, diverging side-path which ascended the
knoll, or round and isolated rock known as Craigellon.

The weather was warm—even sultry. Hesbia
had on a white piqué, striped with green; a black
lace shawl floated over her shoulders, a most knowing
and piquante little hat, with a gleaming bird of
Paradise-plume added to the natural charm of her
soft, bright face.

Hesbia was intensely curious to learn *what*
Lennard wished to say to her so particularly and
so secretly, too !

Did it concern Travice, of whom she had so many
suspicions; or did he mean at last to make a formal
proposal to her ? The beating of her heart increased as she surmised thus to herself.

Until she finds that she is about to lose a lover,
a coquette like Hesbia Vere never knows how much
she might have learned to like him ; and now that
Lennard Blair was about to be sent to South
America for an indefinite period — there seemed

something unpleasantly vague in the locality and term of his absence—he acquired a new and enhanced interest in her eyes. She had questioned her sleek and somewhat taciturn papa about it, and he fully confirmed the information conveyed in Lennard's note; and so quite a gush of sympathy for the poor fellow welled up in her heart—for she was thoroughly a sensationist by nature; and that she might look well in this—perhaps their parting interview—she hung in her pretty white ears a pair of beautiful gold and pearl pendants, which Sir Cullender had presented to her with great formality at breakfast that morning.

Whatever Lennard had to say to her must be of interest—must be odd—strange, she thought, and would be certain to take a very lover-like tone; of that she had no doubt, and the conviction and anticipation gave a lustre to her eye, a colour to her cheek, and a springiness to her step.

" He looks so well when making love, with his dark and earnest eyes," she murmured, for all Lennard's love and adoration had been implied hitherto, and not declared; for the doubts and difficulties, the dread and timidity that withheld a declaration and fettered his tongue were known to himself alone. Hesbia looked at her watch.

" Ten minutes from nine ! "

She could not stay long at the stile; but then, as Lennard would of course be waiting there, he would accompany her homeward along the road, and through the lawn to the garden gate, to prevent the possible locking of which, and to secure her retreat, she had, with much forethought, put the key in her pocket.

The black, flinty brow of Craigellon, fringed with the yellow bells of the beautiful broom, rose against the clear and opal-tinted sky. She could see the path that wound over the grassy upland slope towards it, between two tall cedars; she could also see the old, well-worn and mossy stile, but Lennard Blair was nowhere in sight.

This was scarcely courteous.

If he came as a lover he should certainly have been there before her; so Hesbia paused, looked around, and then proceeded at a much slower pace than she had hitherto adopted. To be first at the trysting-place would never do.

She listened; all was still, but the cawing of the rooks as they winged their way homeward to the old coppice or the ruined church of St. John of Jerusalem. Not a footfall broke the silence. The calmness of evening—the soft, balmy gloaming—lay over everything. The trees were assuming a bronze tint; the wavy line of the Pentland Hills, was deepening from russet green to purple and indigo blue, and their glens were darker still.

Save in the west, where the crimson flush of the set sun lingered beyond Clackmannan, the sky was all of an opal tint that blended with azure as the twinkling stars came out, and the air was full of fragrance; for near the stile, which Hesbia now had reached, there was a grove of balsam pines and silver firs, which were old and decaying, and the breeze, as it passed through them, seemed to be laden with the perfume of the strawberry and pine-apple.

All unused to the most petty disappointment or delay, Hesbia felt extremely annoyed on seeing no sign of Lennard's approach; and now her tiny gold watch indicated that the time was three minutes past nine—decidedly past!

The place was lonely, and the great cedars by the stile cast a gloom over all the place. They were trees of vast age, and were said to have been raised from the seeds of those that grew at Lebanon, brought from the distant East long, long ago, by some pious and valiant Brother of St. John of Torphichen—tradition avers by Sir William Knollys, Lord of St. John, who fell by King James's side at Flodden; for the whole district, like every other in broad Scotland, teems with old, old memories, that even the railroad fails to obliterate.

The flames from the works at the coal-pits on the mains of Kaims now flared out upon the deepening sky at times, and Hesbia felt that she could not, with propriety, loiter where she was much longer.

What was she to say if he proposed?

One may have the thoughts, but how seldom has one the right words to say at the proper time! Should she accept him? Poor Lennard! at that very moment, over their "quiet weed," in the great stately avenue yonder, perhaps her papa and the unhealthy-looking baronet were casting her horoscope—her future—after a very different fashion of their own.

Always attracted most by externals, the finished cut of Lennard's coat, whatever its fashion, his choice of vests, his perfect gloves, and a certain courtliness of manner which he inherited from his father, a modulation of voice and soft expression of eye when addressing ladies in general, and herself in particular, had always led Hesbia to admire and like him.

At that moment there came through the air a strange, weird cry—almost a shriek, that made her shudder. Unlike any sound she had ever heard before, it seemed as the voice of one in mortal anguish and agony. Shrilly it came towards her on the breeze of the darkening evening! She listened intently, but as no other sound followed she returned to her own thoughts.

"What can detain him after all our fuss, secrecy and assignation?" she exclaimed, with impatience that bordered on anger, as she tapped the steps of the stile with her parasol. "He must have misunderstood all about my letter and will no doubt be sending me some crayons to-morrow! Would that I had been plainer, less mysterious; but it is not like Lennard to be so provokingly stupid!"

His absence, unless he had been suddenly seized by illness, seemed to Hesbia totally unaccountable. What could have happened?

An accident! He did not ride, and she knew that he was without horses. That distant and wailing cry had made her heart stand still!

A dread came over her now. Intent upon her own thoughts she had not perceived how much the shadows had deepened, and how gloomy the great cedars made the pathway by the stile.

Somehow she felt inclined to take note, with strange and intense acuteness, of all the features of the now sombre landscape; the number of steps in the stile—there were four, worn, hollow, and spotted with yellow lichens; the forms of the stones in the rough field dyke; the hedgerows, the chirping of the last swallow as it went to its nest; a hawk winging its flight sharply across the clear, calm sky, over which the darkness was stealing like an impalpable tide.

A quarter to ten by the tiny watch; ten minutes —five minutes to ten, and still no appearance of Lennard Blair! To remain longer was unseemly—absurd; and, in perplexity and alarm, she arose and hurried home, while the dew was falling heavily.

Unseen she crossed the lawn, reached the garden,

entered the house, and went straight to her own room, when Mademoiselle Savonette, who alone had been cognizant of her absence, informed her that " M'sieur Sheetwood had come home about an hour since—quite unwell—*malade*—*indisposé*, and had retired to his bed."

Hesbia paid little attention to this information at the time; but there came an occasion when she recalled it unpleasantly to memory. She felt some alarm—for the cry she had heard haunted her; but she felt a great deal more surprise and anger.

Mademoiselle Savonette saw that her mistress was seriously ruffled; but, suspecting a meeting with " M'sieur Blair " as the cause thereof, she was too discreet a Frenchwoman to make any unnecessary remarks, while dressing Hesbia's masses of chesnut-coloured hair for the night.

CHAPTER XXIII.

IN THE TWILIGHT.

TO the beauty of the evening, and the soft charms of the surrounding landscape, rendered so lovely by the mingling of wood and stream, of farm and meadow, with the bolder mountain scenery over all, Travice Cheatwood was totally insensible, as he walked onward with feverish impatience and uncertain step.

The tower of the village church—a structure old as the days when its founder, David, the Scottish Justinian, sat at the gate of his castle of Edinburgh, to administer justice and relieve the wants of the poor—stood up in dark and solid outline against the radiating glory of the setting sun, of which it seemed for a time the focus.

Cheatwood apologized to his conscience, or sought to stifle his selfish fear for the result of the crime he intended to commit, by a steady review of his own desperate fortune; by nursing or fanning his wrath

against Lennard for the card-exposure, till it assumed
the proportions of a deadly and wanton wrong; by a
knowledge of the imperative necessity that no meeting or revelation should take place, as he knew the
dangerous pride of Hesbia, the frail tenure of her
friendship for him, and her decided preference for
Lennard Blair: yet he flattered himself that he only
meant to maim—not kill—his rival, though in reality
not caring much, whatever the result, provided he
was neither discovered nor suspected; and he believed
that no one was aware of his possessing a weapon so
dangerous and illegal as that with which he was
armed; though, by some means, during a visit to his
rooms at Blairavon, Mr. Dabchick had become cognizant of the circumstance.

Travice was not without fears that, by having to
proceed in an entirely opposite direction, in obedience
to Hesbia's wily message, he might miss Lennard,
and that the interview, every way so fatal to his interest and credit, might, after all, take place.

He had thus, first to get rid of the music entrusted
to his charge, that he might, if necessary, have the
means of proving that, at the time the event occurred,
he was in a direction quite away from Craigellon—
where, doubtless, the lovers would linger long enough,
and where he was resolved, if he could steal upon
them unperceived, that he would shoot down Blair,
even if he stood by Hesbia's side; and as he hurried
on towards the Haughs, Travice longed for the meet-

ing, and felt a wild, a desperate, and clamorous
anxiety to get through the last and worst of what he
knew to be a dark, a disreputable—and, that which
was worse than all, personally—a dangerous affair!

He looked at his watch as he walked along the
cool and shady road, which was bordered by high
hedgerows and old trees, the intertwined foliage of
which rustled pleasantly in the passing breeze. The
sun had set beyond the mountains; the old tower
of the village church seemed darker than ever, and
sharper in outline. Twilight was stealing on, and
in half an hour the meeting would take place at the
stile.

At the gate-lodge of the Haughs he delivered the
roll of music, with one of his cards, for Miss Cheyne,
muttering to the keeper something about " the
sultry state of the weather," probably as an expla-
nation of his flushed and somewhat disordered appearance; and then hastened to reach a lane which
led, he knew, through the fields towards the place
of meeting, grasping with feverish impatience his
weapon as he went.

To those who know not what it is, we may explain
that an air-gun has two barrels, one *inside* the
other, the inner being of necessity of a smaller
bore; down these the balls are put by means of a
ramrod like that of any muzzle-loader, and from
thence they are expelled. A syringe is fixed in the
stock of the gun, by which the air is injected into

the cavity between the external and central barrels. Another valve, on being opened by the trigger, permits the condensed air to expel the bullet, which comes forth without sound, but with deadly force. If this valve be opened and. shut suddenly, one charge of condensed air will suffice for the discharge of several balls; but if the whole is emitted at once, the force of expulsion is great indeed.

"I've seen many a sensation drama (Travice never read novels, as he hated them), but, by Jove! I never thought to figure in one," he muttered through his clenched teeth, as he wiped the clammy perspiration from his face and ears.

Ere reaching the lane which diverges at a right angle from the highway and leads westward to Craigellon—being, in fact, but a continuation of the same path which Hesbia was traversing from the eastward to reach the stile, a central point—Travice heard footsteps, and his heart leaped painfully for a moment, and then for another seemed to stand still, when the figure of Lennard Blair, there — *there* where he least expected to meet him, crossed the road and entered the footway before him.

The truth was that Lennard had been sharing a farewell dinner with Doctor Feverley, at the latter's little cottage in the hamlet, and was now hastening, with a light and hopeful heart, to keep his tryst with Hesbia—a last, and to him it might prove a most important one.

Travice sprang forward; not a second was to be lost—his game, his victim, his rival was before him, in sight, in range; but Travice was rendered for a brief time powerless by a sudden and painful but spasmodic contraction of the heart, by a singing in his ears, and a species of blindness that came upon him.

The grass was growing rank and deep in the old and unfrequented path, so the footsteps of the victim and the destroyer were alike muffled, as the latter glided after the former, whose figure loomed darkly against the twilight of the west; then Travice levelled his weapon, and aiming low — intent to wound, but not to kill—pulled the trigger!

There was a sound like a hiss as the ball was shot; then Lennard uttered the wild cry that was heard by Hesbia—one of agony, as if struck in a vital part: he threw up his arms, and fell heavily on his back.

Travice saw this, but he saw no more. He forced a passage through a dense and thorny hedge, tearing his hands and clothes in the process, and, dashing into a coppice, rushed away by what he conceived to be the nearest route to Blairavon.

Through the deep rank fern, the lair of the deer and the hare; over water-courses and rivulets; over sunk fences, stone walls, and turf dykes; across fields of sprouting corn and wheat, he ran, with a peed he never thought to exert, stumbling, falling,

rising, and plunging, as if pursued by something
unseen, and with a mortal terror in his heart—a
terror that came upon him the moment he pulled
the fatal trigger.

Bathed in perspiration, weak as a child, feeble
and trembling in every limb and fibre, he was compelled at times to pause, to lie on the cool earth,
and recover breath and the power of further volition.
Then, through the singing in his ears and the
memory of Lennard's cry, there seemed an awful,
a preternatural, a dead stillness in the air of the
summer evening. His heart beat madly, painfully;
there was still the old clamorous anxiety about it;
but added thereto was a gnawing terror of the
future, of suspicion and discovery. The very trees
that cast their gloom upon his path seemed as if
they were mute witnesses against him; the stars in
the sky, as they came twinkling out one by one,
were as eyes observant of the new and terrible crime
he had committed—for might not Blair be dead!

He would have given worlds—years of his life—
to know that Lennard was only wounded, not dead
—not dead; but he dared not go back to look; he
must away—away to conceal himself, and escape, if
he could, the alarm and, perhaps, detection of the
morrow.

Away—but to where?

Cunning rather than wisdom suggested that to
pass unseen into Blairavon House, to get to bed and

feign an illness, were his best plans; and he staggered wearily on, to put them into execution.

The extra bullets with which he had provided
himself he threw far into a cornfield; there, if ever
found, they would lie at least unseen till harvest-
time. He feared to cast away the air-gun, lest it
should give a clue to the committal of the crime;
and he knew not where to conceal it.

In the root of a tree—none were hollow; in a
rabbit-hole—none was near; to bury it might only
lead to its certain discovery by the disturbance of
the earth; in the bed of the trouting-stream it
might be found by the first fisherman who came
whipping the water with his line; in a ditch it
might be discovered by the first truant-boy who
came bird-nesting or some ploughman going afield:
of all such instances he had heard or read in trials
and at inquests held by coroners. There were no
such officials in Scotland; but he knew that in each
county was a Procurator Fiscal, the terror of whose
name—there was something foreign in the sound of
it—he now felt fully for the first time; and with
this came visions of arrest, of shame and imprisonment, of trial and suffering—even of Calcraft, that
finisher of the law, so cold and stern, white-haired
and inexorable!

Thus instead of casting away the weapon he took
it home with him, though he had sundry vague
ideas of leaving it in some one's house or room,

that on *them* might fall the suspicion and the punishment; his remorse for the murder, if such it was, being quite secondary to his terror of personal implication in the deed.

Why, oh why had he not yielded to the occasional better impulses which had prompted him to cast away this deadly but silent weapon, the tempter to a crime like this?

He had read or heard of men—yea, and of women, too—who, after such an act, felt as if the crime, the sense of being a destroyer, added to their own secret importance; who felt actually elevated in the conviction that they had sent an immortal soul from earth on its long, long journey.

Amid all the wild incoherence of his thoughts— the sense as if his mind wandered among cliffs and pitfalls, precipices and caverns; places of dread, and doubt, and danger—no such emotion as this occurred to him.

It was all misery and fear—intense and selfish fear!

As he staggered through the vestibule and up the staircase of Blairavon House, leaning on what appeared to be a thick walking-staff, but which was actually the means of the crime he had just perpetrated, his pale and wretched appearance excited the surprise of Mademoiselle Savonette, to whom he muttered something of being ill, and to send the butler to him as he required some brandy-and-water, and then he reached once more his own room.

An age seemed to have elapsed since he had left it!

"Candles?" no; he did not require them—his head was throbbing and his eyes could not bear the light; but the brandy-and-water he drunk with the thirst of one who might have been in the Black Hole at Calcutta. How his teeth chattered against the rummer, and how grateful was the ice which the thoughtful butler had dropped into it!

Then, by chance, his eyes fell upon a mirror. He started back on beholding the ghastly pallor of his own face, which seemed white as that of a spectre in the twilight.

It was no longer like his own; it had a dark scowl upon it, and he drew fearfully and doubtfully closer, to assure himself that it was really a reflection and not the spectrum of *another*. His chest was heaving, and the bead-drops of a cold perspiration were on his temples. He concealed the air-gun between the mattresses of his bed for a time, and after placing his tremulous hands upon his brow, as if he would compress his brain and recall his scattered energies, he muttered,—

"To bed—to bed! I must not be seen thus!"

Then, hastily undressing, he tied up for future concealment or destruction the suit he had worn that evening, sprang into bed and buried his face

among the pillows; but a new terror seized him—
that he might become really ill; and, if a fever, conduced by his past potations and present terrible
emotions, came upon him, he might, in his delirium,
reveal, and so bear witness against himself.

"Let me be calm—be calm, or I shall go mad!"
he muttered again and again, while striving to
reason quietly on the chances for and against the
death of his victim and the hazards of discovery.
Strange to say, the latter seemed to grow less; and,
after reviewing all the features of his position, the
prospect appeared more re-assuring—or was it an
insane and defiant recklessness that possessed him?

Amid it all, in his ears and in his soul was the
echo of a terrible cry, and he seemed to see a human
figure lying on its back, in that dark and lonely
path, with pallid face, with fallen jaw, and stony
eyes that stared at the silent stars!

END OF VOLUME FIRST.

WYMAN AND SONS, PRINTERS, GREAT QUEEN STREET, LONDON, W.C.